"My Brain Takes Precedence Over My Body—And It Says No, Loud And Clear."

Lisa placed her hands on Carson's chest and gave a slight push to let him know she meant it. "I need the whole shot. The little cottage where the roses bloom. Two cats in the yard. A swing set out back."

Carson drew away. "And a little white crib in the nursery. So, the way I see it, you still believe in fairy tales."

Lisa flashed him a quick smile. "Happy endings? Absolutely."

"Then if we put this into fairy-tale terms..." Carson began.

"You are the big bad wolf," Lisa finished for him.

He looked downright shocked. "But I always thought of myself as the handsome prince!"

Lisa laughed. "Think again."

Dear Reader,

When I think of autumn, I think of cool, crisp November nights curled up by the fire . . . reading a red-hot Silhouette Desire novel. Now, I know not all of you live in cooler climes, but I'm sure you, too, can conjure up visions of long, cozy nights with the hero of your dreams.

Speaking of heroes, Dixie Browning has created a wonderful one in MacCasky Ford, the hero of her *Man of the Month* book, *Not a Marrying Man*. Mac is a man you'll never forget, and he certainly meets his match in Banner Keaton.

November is also a time of homecoming, and Leslie Davis Guccione has been "away from home" for far too long. I know everyone will be glad to see her back with *A Gallant Gentleman*. And if you're looking for something tender, provocative and inspirational, don't miss Ashley Summer's *Heart's Ease*. This story is one I feel very strongly about, and I'd be interested in hearing how you like it.

Rounding out November are a delicious love story from Raye Morgan, *Baby Aboard*, a fiery romp by Carole Buck, *Red-Hot Satin*, and a sexy, spritely tale by Karen Leabo, *Lindy and the Law*.

So, until next month, happy reading!

Lucia Macro
Senior Editor

RAYE MORGAN

BABY ABOARD

SILHOUETTE *Desire*®

Published by Silhouette Books New York

America's Publisher of Contemporary Romance

SILHOUETTE BOOKS
300 East 42nd St., New York, N.Y. 10017

BABY ABOARD

Copyright © 1991 by Helen Conrad

ISBN: 0-373-05673-7

First Silhouette Books printing November 1991

Printed in the U.S.A.

Books by Raye Morgan

Silhouette Desire

Embers of the Sun #52
Summer Wind #101
Crystal Blue Horizon #141
A Lucky Streak #393
Husband for Hire #434
Too Many Babies #543
Ladies' Man #562
In a Marrying Mood #623
Baby Aboard #673

Silhouette Romance

Roses Never Fade #427

RAYE MORGAN

favors settings in the West, which is where she has spent most of her life. She admits to a penchant for Western heroes, believing that whether he's a rugged outdoorsman or a smooth city sophisticate, he tends to have a streak of wildness that the romantic heroine can't resist taming. She's been married to one of those Western men for twenty years and is busy raising four more in her Southern California home.

One

"Check your baby right here, please."

Lisa Loring looked from the woman in the bright pink uniform to the group of babies, each one in its own little molded plastic carrier with large handles, lined up on the conveyor belt. There must have been fifty of them, all smiling and cooing as they bobbed along.

"Where are they going?" she heard herself ask in a faraway voice.

"Your baby will be returned to you immediately," the uniformed woman told her kindly. "Just walk through the metal detector, and your baby will be inside waiting for you in the lobby." She smiled again. "Where is your baby? You need to check your baby now."

Lisa turned and fidgeted with the hem of her jacket. She was carrying something, but it didn't seem to be a baby. "I...I don't know where my baby is," she answered worriedly.

"Oh, dear," said Pinky. "I'm afraid you must be in the wrong line."

There was a murmur from behind. The other women in the line, each holding a plastic carrier with a baby inside, began to repeat the phrase. "She's in the wrong line. Oh, dear, she's in the wrong line."

"I'm sorry, miss," Pinky told her sadly. "You're in the wrong line. You'll have to go over there."

Lisa looked in the direction that Pinky was pointing. Another line stretched through the building—a line of women in handsome wool business suits. "Check your briefcase right here," the attendant for that line was saying. "It will be returned to you in the lobby."

Lisa looked down and sure enough, her scarlet-tipped fingers were curled around the handle of a briefcase. "I guess I'll have to go to the other line," she told the others sadly. "I'm sorry."

They shook their heads in sympathy. "No, we're sorry," Pinky corrected. "Please come back if you decide to change lines."

Lisa walked toward the other line, but the faster she walked, the farther away it got. She started running, but the briefcase was too heavy and she had to drop it. She was running harder and harder, panting now, trying with all her might. But the line had disappeared. She turned, looking all around, but there was no one else in sight. She was alone.

Suddenly a bell rang. She covered her ears and closed her eyes, but the bell kept ringing. It was going to ring forever, unless...

Lisa's flailing hand finally found the alarm clock and slapped down the button to stop the ringing. Yawning, she stretched back against the pillows and slowly forced her eyes open. Outside it was still dark, but there was a purple tinge to the edge of the horizon. The sun was about to make an appearance.

She focused her mind and shuddered. Another baby dream. This was becoming ridiculous.

Why couldn't she make up her mind what she really wanted? Tomorrow would be her thirty-fifth birthday. Her body was handing her a deadline she couldn't ignore. The question she'd managed to avoid for the past fifteen-plus years while she was building her career in department-store management was finally staring her in the face. Was she going to have a baby, or wasn't she?

It was a terrifying question. Maybe that was why she'd hesitated for so long. If she said no, a thousand doors would suddenly slam shut. Just the thought of it tore at her in a way that made her want to cry out. But if she said yes... In some ways that was even more frightening.

Fumbling, she turned on her bedside lamp and blinked in the pool of light that flooded her. She was back in the same room she had slept in as a child. Redecoration and new furniture had wiped out a lot of memories. But it did have a warm and comforting familiarity to it just the same. It would be easy to lie back in that comfort and ignore reality. But she didn't have any easy time left. That was over. It was now, or very likely never.

To make matters worse, this whole decision thing was coming at a very awkward time. Here she was, back in the hometown she had deserted when she was eighteen, a little overwhelmed by the house and business her recently deceased grandfather had left her. She needed all her energies to focus on fighting hard to keep her family's department store from going under. The struggle was consuming her every waking moment. And yet...there it was.

Yes, she couldn't deny it. Forget logic. Forget being sensible. She wanted a baby.

She looked about at the huge brass bed she lay in. The covers were clean and white and fluffy. It was a delicious bed to sleep in. But it was a very empty bed; one that was made for two, but was only being used by one.

It was all very well to lie here and moan about wanting a baby. There did seem to be a step in the process missing, however. Before she could have a baby, she needed a husband.

"Just one little husband," she murmured to the huge yellow chrysanthemums that covered her walls as she pushed her silver-blond hair back out of her eyes. "I don't need a hero. I don't need looks or wealth or power. Just make him a nice guy. Is that too much to ask?"

Apparently so. She hadn't found anyone to handle the job in a lot of years of looking. Not that there hadn't been applicants. At first she'd been beating them off with a stick. But lately, as she'd gotten more and more immersed in her career, the eligible men had faded away, until she suddenly realized it had been a year since she'd had a date with a man she even liked very much.

No dates meant no husband, and no husband meant no baby.

Downstairs the ancient grandfather clock began to toll the hour, its chimes echoing through the big old empty house. She groaned. No more time for regrets. She had a job to get to. Loring's Department Store was waiting to be saved from ruin.

She swung her feet to the floor, staring at the leather briefcase sitting in the chair beside her bed. Hadn't her dream been something about briefcases? She couldn't quite get it clear in her mind. Shaking her head, she got up and headed for the shower, thinking, another fun-filled busy day ahead.

"And...who knows?" she muttered as she turned on the water. "Maybe today I'll meet the man of my dreams."

Carson James pulled himself up out of the water and vaulted onto the side of the condominium's swimming pool, sitting for a moment to catch his breath and let the water drain off. The spring morning was cool, but he'd worked hard swimming laps and his body temperature was high. Had the exercise done him any good? It was hard to tell. He hadn't had much sleep the night before and despite the healthy workout, right now he felt as if someone had used his head for wool storage.

Flexing his wide shoulders, he grimaced. It was one thing to end up this way after a night of hard partying. It was quite another to feel like corn mush was running in your veins because the baby next door had cried all night long. He had no happy memories, just desperate thoughts of revenge.

"Here. Catch."

He looked up just in time to see the thick blue towel coming at him. Reaching out he plucked it from the air.

"Thanks," he said, smiling briefly at the pretty young woman who had tossed it to him. Sally, he thought her name was. She shared a condo with a couple of other single women. Rising to his feet, he began to dry off.

"You're welcome."

She was dressed for work, yet she hesitated for a moment, as if hoping for an invitation to a more lengthy chat. But Carson wasn't in a talkative mood, and he didn't offer her an opening. Lingering a bit longer, she didn't try to hide the fact that she was enjoying the picture he made with silver streams of water reflecting the early-morning sunlight on his tanned and well-toned flesh. His shoulders were solid and muscular, his hips taut and barely concealed by the strip of bright blue Lycra he wore. As he bent to begin drying the dark, crisp hair on his long legs, she made a small gurgling noise deep in her throat, shook herself, and started off toward the condominium parking garage.

"See you later," she called back hopefully.

"What?" Carson looked after her. "Oh. Sure. See you."

But he had hardly noticed her presence. His mind was groggy from lack of sleep and filled with one driving urge: It was time. He looked toward the horizon, toward where the sea met the sky. That wanderlust was stirring in him once again. He had to get out of this place and move on to something new.

"Hey, mister. Mister?"

Startled, he looked down to find a small person tugging on his towel. He frowned, his wet hair falling over his forehead. He thought this was an adults-only condominium development. Lately there had been all too many children around.

This one was short and serious, with dark, almond-shaped eyes and jet-black hair cut like a close-fitting cap around her head.

"Mister, can you help me get my cat?"

A cat, too? Pets weren't allowed, either. Carson wanted to swear, but he couldn't—not in front of a child. That was one more thing to hold against them.

"Where is your cat?" he asked reluctantly, still frowning.

The little girl stared at him with unblinking eyes. "He's up in the tree. Can't you hear him?"

Now that she mentioned it, of course he could hear the caterwauling. Turning, he saw a ginger-colored feline caught up in the Chinese elm, clinging to a branch and wailing pitifully. He probably hadn't noticed before, he told himself grouchily, because his hearing was still impaired from an entire night spent listening to that baby cry.

He'd seen this little girl going in and out of the condo next door. Jan, his neighbor, had said her sister was coming to stay for a while, but she had neglected to mention that her sister came with some very noisy baggage.

"Do you have a baby in your family?" he asked the little girl suspiciously.

She nodded with no hesitation. "Tammy is our baby."

"Does she cry all the time?"

She nodded again. "She's teething. Mom tries to keep her quiet, but she just cries and cries. Mom says if we don't be quiet, some mean person will turn us in to the manager and they'll kick us out."

He stared at her hard for a moment. "Mom could be right," he said under his breath, reaching for his robe. But he knew he was bluffing. He'd been tempted at two in the morning, as the baby wailed, one thin wall away. He'd made plans of revenge, had pictured the entire family on the street sitting atop their possessions. But when it came right down to it, he knew he wasn't going to do it. He stifled a yawn. No. He would just lose sleep and endure....

Another good reason to move on, he told himself as he looked toward the tree. The signs were right. It was time to go.

He picked up his watch from the wrought-iron poolside table. It was still an hour before he had to be in at work, but he did want to run by Loring's Department Store today and get a fix on what was going on there. Well, he could do that later. Turning, he looked at the little girl. Usually he was immune to cute kiddy scenes other people oohed and aahed over. But this urchin seemed to have a special built-in appeal. Even he would have a hard time resisting the plea in those big brown eyes.

"Okay," he told her gruffly. "I'll get your cat down."

"Thank you," she said, trotting along beside him as he set off on his quest.

Stopping at the foot of the tree, he looked up at the cat and sighed. Climbing a tree in a swimsuit was not his idea of a very bright thing to do, but he didn't seem to have much choice.

"What's your name, kid?" he asked the child.

"Michi Ann Nakashima. And my cat is called Jake."

"Okay, Michi Ann Nakashima. I'll make you a deal. I'll go up and get your cat, if you ask your mother to move the baby into a room on the other side of the condo tonight. Okay?"

She stared at him solemnly, not saying a word.

"The baby cries," he explained. "I can't sleep."

She got it. She nodded wisely. "Okay," she replied. "It's a deal." This was one bright little girl. You could almost like a kid like this.

"Right." He was almost cheerful now. After all, he was going to be a hero, at least to one scrawny cat and one little brown-eyed girl. Not a bad way to start the day. "Here goes." And he began climbing hand over hand, up into the tree. All he could see above him was a ginger-colored blur and a row of very sharp, white teeth. "Here, kitty," he called as he moved toward it. "Nice kitty. I'm going to save you."

Lisa sat in the huge office and looked around herself with a sense of wonder and not a little dread. This was it: the inner sanctum, the royal throne where her grandfather had held sway for all the years of her childhood. And now she was sitting in the seat of power.

It seemed strange, unnatural.

"It's downright creepy," she muttered aloud, glaring up at the portrait of the old man.

But even from the great beyond, he defeated her, staring her down as he always had. She looked away and heard her own voice mumbling "Sorry," before she could stop herself.

She had been back for almost a month now, taking charge of Loring's Department Store. But somehow she had avoided actually sitting in the huge old chair until now—sitting right where he had sat when he had ordered her to give up those frivolous piano lessons; to stop seeing that unsuitable boy, Dougie Switzer; to stay in town and go to junior college instead of following this crazy dream of going to school in the East.

She had obeyed every order up to that last one. At eighteen, with a head full of ideas and a heart full of resentment, she'd packed up and taken off into the night, hating her grandfather for the way he was forcing her to do it.

It was only now, almost seventeen years later, that she thought she understood how much he had loved this town and this family-owned store, and how much he had wanted her to love it all, too.

Her grandfather had died three weeks before, but he had called her home in time for a bittersweet reunion, taking it for granted that she would take over the store. And suddenly, a concept she had scorned for years had become unavoidable.

Was she ready for this job? She glanced at her own reflection in the window across the room, hoping for confirmation of her grown-up state. And she got it. What she saw was a poised, attractive woman in a beige business suit, who had a confident set to her shoulders and wore a Loring's badge that simply read Lisa—an idea of her own to quickly help put her on equal terms with the store employees.

Taking a deep breath, she looked straight at the portrait once more. "I'm all grown-up, Grandfather," she said softly. "And I'm ready."

To her dismay, her eyes were suddenly brimming with tears.

The shrill sound of the telephone interrupted her thoughts and she reached gratefully for the receiver, wiping away the moisture and managing a professional response.

"Miss Loring? This is Krissi, in Perfumes and Cosmetics?" The girl's voice was high and her tone conspiratorial. "Remember I told you about that guy who was snooping around yesterday? Well, he's back."

Lisa sat up, alert and interested. "Thanks, Krissi," she said briskly. "I'll be right down."

Rocketing out of her chair, she marched toward the elevator, her dark eyes gleaming. From what Krissi had told her yesterday, she had a hunch what this fellow was up to. For as long as she could remember, Loring's had been locked in a tug-of-war with Kramer's Department Store, across the street. So now Mike Kramer was sending spies over to find out what was going on under the new administration, was he? Well, she would just see about that.

She found Krissi flattened against a wall, peering around a corner.

"Here he comes, Miss Loring. He's heading for the Bridal Shoppe," said the salesgirl.

She was hissing through her braces, motioning for Lisa to follow her behind a row of mannequins dressed as brides and grooms. Crouching down, her shoulders hunched high around her frizzy permed hair, Krissi did a fine imitation of a police detective as she slunk her way to a prime vantage point.

Lisa raised an eyebrow at Krissi's theatrics, but she followed just the same. She drew the line at slinking, but she did try to remain inconspicuous behind the folds of a voluminous satin wedding dress, peering out to catch the spy in action.

"There he is!"

And there he was, brow furrowed and pencil poised, just as Krissi had said, gazing at each display in turn and jotting down notes.

"He's spying for Kramer's," Krissi whispered, her eyes wide behind her horn-rimmed glasses. "I'll just bet he is. What do you think?"

Lisa hesitated before stating her opinion. She would hate to accuse anyone unjustly. But the man staring raptly at the white satin and lace hardly looked like a customer for the Bridal Shoppe. His charcoal-gray suit was impeccable and his white shirt starched, but he moved like an athlete and had the rugged face of a street fighter. He really was just the sort Mike Kramer would hire to come over to scope out the competition.

"Want me to call Security?" Krissi asked hopefully.

Lisa shook her head, resigned. "No, Krissi. You go on back to the perfume counter. I'll handle this."

The girl's chubby cheeks sagged with disappointment. "Maybe I should stay around as backup," she suggested in a last-ditch effort. "Just in case he gets rough."

Lisa's smile was quick and genuine. "He's not going to get rough. This is just retailing, Krissi. Not *On the Waterfront*."

"Well, okay." Krissi threw one last, lingering look at the man still scribbling things into his notebook. "I guess I'll go on back to work."

Lisa waited until Krissi had turned the corner and then she sighed. She had no idea what she was going to say to the spy. She'd never had to deal with this sort of thing when she was working as floor manager at Bartholomew's in New York. Only in small towns did you seem to find competition this personal, like feuds between families.

As she watched, he pulled out a small recorder and began speaking into it in a voice too low for her to hear. Ideas, no doubt, for Mike.

Outrage surged through her. Loring's was having a hard enough time making ends meet without this new assault from Kramer's. How dare that man send snoops right into her store? All hesitation melted away and she stepped briskly forward to confront the spy.

Carson had a headache, a pending deadline and a stomach that was growling over yet another missed lunch. So why, he was asking himself with wonder, had he decided to stop in at Loring's again in order to get this next assignment rolling, even though he was up against it on the Covington Electronics deal?

He was getting to be a workaholic, that was the reason. And it was ridiculous. He had always prided himself on being a free spirit, tied down by nothing, ready to change direction with the wind. And here he was, so engrossed in his job with Central Coast Bank that he had been in this sleepy little beach town for over a year.

Basically, it was fascinating work. He went into companies about to default on their bank loans and advised them on renovations, restructuring, and streamlining techniques that often turned their fortunes around. He'd originally taken the job on a whim, and had been amazed at how much he enjoyed the work. But it certainly had put him into a rut. He was beginning to feel restless, and the feeling was intensifying. It was time to move on.

This Loring's job was going to be a tough one. He knew the type—old family, terrified of change. They would resist his recommendations. And they would go under. It was written in the stars. Just a few times scouting around had told him that. It hardly seemed worth the effort.

He said as much into his recorder in a few terse sentences, then turned with a frown to watch a saleswoman approach, shoving the little machine into his jacket pocket. She was lovely enough to capture his attention, even in the fine state of annoyance he found himself. Her silver-blond hair was pulled back into a bun, but a generous wave was left free to fall provocatively over her forehead, and her clear dark eyes were rimmed with thick dark lashes that set off their warm glow. She was dressed like something out of a very expensive women's magazine, wearing a cream-colored suit of some wool blend that looked soft as a San Francisco fog, and a bronze silk blouse with a small, neat ruffle at the throat, held by a simple gold pin. On one lapel was her identity nameplate. It merely read Lisa.

His first thought was that he hadn't seen such a beautiful woman this close for a very long time. His second thought, from a mind still entrenched in business, was that the saleswomen at Loring's must be too well-paid if they could afford a dress like this one.

The one thought was off-the-wall, a symptom of how fuzzy his mind was getting from overwork. A sense of the reaction he would get if he suggested reducing all Loring's salaries flashed through his mind. He would certainly be the most unpopular man in town. The corners of his mouth tilted into something almost resembling a smile as he nodded to the woman who had just approached him.

Lisa, however, was not amused. She stopped before him and fixed him with a challenging glance that somewhat surprised him. Women often looked at him, but they weren't usually so cool and judgmental. This was interesting. He waited, wondering what she wanted.

What Lisa wanted was for him to look a little guilty. She would prefer it if he would actually turn and run for the exit, but barring that, a little chagrin would do. He was the crook, after all, and should show some shame. Instead, she was getting humor, and that offended her. He looked like a tough guy, but not anything she couldn't handle. She was used to dealing with men. He didn't scare her a bit.

"And just what are you doing here?" she asked with a wave of her hand, her dark eyes bright with challenge.

"Who me?" He was surprised by the inappropriateness of such a question from a saleswoman. He looked around as though at a loss, then turned his gaze back to meet hers.

"Yes, you."

She looked so fierce, he almost grinned.

"I'm browsing. What are you doing here?" he countered.

"I work here," she responded with a toss of her head.

He nodded slowly, holding back his smile. "I can see that." She had a lovely face—creamy skin, a slender nose, huge eyes the color of rich Brazilian coffee. Looking at her reminded him of a spring day in the South when the dogwood was blooming. But there was a strength in her face that belied the soft, satin image.

"Well, you see," he told her patiently, "you work here. I shop here. That's the way the system is set up. That's why they call it a store."

Lovely as she was, she didn't appreciate his attempt at some light comedy. He could see that right away.

"You don't shop here at all," she told him. "Don't you think I can tell? Let's not play games. I know why you're here."

"That makes two of us." He gazed at her quizzically, wondering what her angle could possibly be. Her attractive qualities were beginning to pale in light of her single-mindedness where goading him was concerned. All his better instincts told him to make tracks. "Now, if you'll excuse me..."

He started to turn away, but she stepped in front of him, her jaw set, her eyes defiant.

"You really think I'm going to stand back and let you sabotage me without doing a thing about it? If I have to, I'll call the police."

"The police." He stared at her, astounded. "Listen, lady, I don't know what you think I'm up to here, but..." He was beginning to have serious doubts about the stability of this saleswoman's mind. It was really too bad, but it seemed to be true that there was always something wrong with the most beautiful ones. It was as though some higher being thought there ought to be at least one flaw in every otherwise-perfect jewel, just so you didn't get too cocky. "What is it? Are you accusing me of shoplifting?"

Her lovely face was stern with disapproval. "You know better."

He blinked at her, at a loss. "Are you this friendly to all your customers?" he asked. "If so, I can see why this store is in trouble."

He turned away again, but she stopped him with a hand on his upper arm.

"Listen," she began, then hesitated as two women shoppers approached where they stood. Still holding his arm, she smiled at them pleasantly, waiting until they had turned in at the next display.

"I know what you're doing here," she whispered to him as soon as the area was clear, her pink fingernails digging into the wool fabric of his jacket as her gaze challenged his. "You're a spy, aren't you?"

"A . . . a spy?" He choked out the words. This was one for the books. And there wasn't a trace of humor in her eyes, so she wasn't joking. "Right," he went on, his voice lightly edged with scorn. "You could see that, could you, even without the trench coat and the dark glasses?"

"It's only obvious," she said defensively. "I've been watching you. I've seen what you're doing."

He nodded slowly, searching her eyes for some clue. This really was crazy. "Okay. I'll accept that. Obviously, I'm a spy." He tried a smile, but no, she didn't smile back. "The question is, what do you do to spies around here? Do you hang them by the toes? Or do I have to wait around for you to assemble a firing squad?"

There was something about the way he was reacting that was rattling her confidence. Could she have made a mistake? "Look," she said quickly, "I know you're just some hireling of Mike's, just trying to make a living. And I really shouldn't take my anger out on you, but . . ."

"Hey." Reaching out, he captured her wrist in his hand. He looked at her evenly and said with calm detachment, "Snap out of it. I am not working for anybody named Mike. I'm not your spy. Honest."

"Oh." But she wasn't reacting to his words. She was looking at his hand on her wrist, startled by the fiery red scratches it was covered with. She looked quickly up into his eyes.

He saw what she had noticed and sighed. "A close encounter of the feline kind," he explained. "Try to do a good deed and you generally end up paying for it."

She hardly heard what he said. She was still looking into his eyes and wishing she hadn't. Blue as the sky on a summer day, they were assessing her in a sensual way that made her blink rather too quickly, and his full lips had a lover's tilt to them that drew her attention, as well. He looked like a playboy to her. That was a type she despised. So why was she feeling this sudden pulse in her throat?

He was by no means handsome in a traditional sense, but the very strength of his maleness was alluring, and she did feel oddly attracted to him. That in itself was disconcerting. She didn't usually respond to men that way. In fact, after many years on the dating scene, she had become very cynical about the male sex as a whole, especially men whom she considered candidates for her attention. It had been a long time since a man had made her breathless.

Not that that was what was happening now, she told herself quickly. It was indignation that was doing it. Nothing more. Taking a deep breath and forcing her gaze away from his, she tried one last ploy.

"Okay. If you're not spying for Mike, prove it. Let me see what you were writing in the little notebook you've got tucked away in your pocket." She raised her chin and glared at him. "Let's take a look."

He released her wrist and made a sound of impatience. "No, let's not," he replied tersely.

"Ah!" The accusation in her voice was clear. "Then, what about that recorder in your jacket pocket? I'll bet you don't dare let me listen in on that, either."

By now he was doing a slow burn. The woman was loony. That was all there was to it. And as far as he was concerned, she could go be loony with someone else. He had things to do.

"You know, Lisa," he said softly, "you're a very beautiful woman, but I'm afraid you're playing with a deck that's a few cards short. Someone is going to have to warn your manager. You really shouldn't be allowed to accost the customers this way.''

She gasped, but he paid no attention. Sighing, he shook his head regretfully, then glanced at his watch. ''But I'm running late. I'm afraid I will have to leave that for another time.''

''Here's a news flash for you, mister,'' she stated firmly, managing to cover up the fact that her pulse was racing and her breath was coming too quickly, and at the same time, wondering how she had managed to lose her legendary composure so easily in this encounter. ''I am the manager. In fact, I manage the entire store. So you'll have to make your complaints directly to me.''

''You're the manager, huh?'' His grin twisted one side of his wide mouth. ''Right. And I'm the spy.'' He sighed and shook his head. ''I've had a great time chatting with you, Lisa. I can't tell you how unique it's been. But the fact is, I've got places I've got to be. I'm afraid you'll have to excuse me.''

He threw one last exasperated look at her, and made his way toward the escalator. Lisa stood very still, watching him go. She ought to call store security. But what good would that do now? He wouldn't be back. He'd been caught in the act.

Still, it hadn't gone quite the way she would have liked, had it? She thought of his blue eyes and shivered. It was fairly disturbing to discover that a man like him seemed to affect her this way. She'd never liked his sort. She was looking for quite a different type of man.

Turning to leave the Bridal Shoppe, she thought about her ideal—the man she was forever searching for—the father of her baby. He would be kind and calm, of course. He would wear tweed jackets with leather patches at the elbows and sit quietly by the fire much of the time, reading from a book of poetry—Robert Browning, most likely. When asked for an opinion, he would frown thoughtfully and think things through before answering. His name would probably be Ted, or William.

She sighed, knowing she was living in dreamland. If there was such a man, he was probably hiding out on some university campus somewhere. And here she was, stuck in a beach town in California, dealing with blue-eyed playboys moonlighting as spies. It hardly seemed likely she was going to find old calm, thoughtful Ted out here in sun country. It hardly seemed likely at all.

Two

___

Blue eyes were nothing, of course. Plenty of men had blue eyes. If that was really what she was after, all she would have to do would be to take a walk along the beach and look at what was riding in on those ubiquitous surf-boards—blue-eyed blonds as far as the eye could see.

No. Looks had nothing to do with it, and neither did blue eyes. It was character she was looking for. Strength. Integrity. Stability.

"A helpmate," she said aloud, strolling back to the elevator en route to her office. "A pal. A protector. A man who doesn't mind changing a diaper or warming a bit of formula once in a while."

"A saint," added a voice from inside her head. "You're looking for a saint in San Feliz. A cultured saint who loves children. Maybe you should set your sights a little lower. After all, you're going to be..."

"Thirty-five," she said aloud. "Yes, I know."

"What was that, Miss Loring?" A pretty dark-haired girl who worked in Juniors looked out brightly from behind her counter.

"Uh...nothing, Chelly. Just talking to myself."

"Oh." Chelly smiled. "Okay, then."

They'll start to think I'm bonkers, she thought as she leaned back against the wall of the elevator and listened to it whirr. I'd better watch out.

She had gotten into the habit of talking to herself. Maybe that was because she felt a bit lonely, without any real friends to talk to. And the work had been so hard, lately. For just a moment, she thought longingly of the old days in New York—the tranquil afternoons spent meeting with floor managers, the leisurely lunches, the entertaining trade shows, the meetings with distributors and designers. She'd exchanged all that for a failing department store where spies roamed the halls and memories of her grandfather haunted her. At the moment, it hardly seemed a good bargain.

The spy. Yes, she was going to have to follow through on that. Mike Kramer was the one she should be facing over this. Thinking of her lifelong enemy, indignation ran strong in her once again.

"Terry, get me Mike Kramer on the phone," she called to her secretary as she passed her desk.

"Sure, Miss Loring."

Lisa turned and shook her head at the young woman. "Call me Lisa," she reminded her—not for the first time.

"Sure, Miss Loring," Terry replied, her green eyes wide, her red curls bouncing as she nodded her head. Lisa shrugged and went into her office, barely glancing at the portrait of her grandfather as she sank into his chair. It was beginning to feel comfortable.

Within seconds, Terry buzzed in with her call.

"Mike?"

"Yeah?" Mike's smart-aleck voice was still familiar from childhood pranks and teasing. She and Mike had always been enemies, even in kindergarten. Though they hadn't come face-to-face since she'd been back, they'd had many a telephone conversation, and she could picture his short, stocky frame and his square face that always wore a demonic grin.

"Mike Kramer, you're a snake in the grass and I'm going to get you back."

He chuckled. The most annoying thing about Mike was that the angrier she got with him, the more he liked it. "Ooh, baby, I love it when you whisper sweet nothings in my ear. What did I do now? Was it really terrible? Are you ready to sell out to me?"

Lisa's shoulders sagged and she couldn't help but smile. She should have known better than to call him. Why did she always fall into his traps?

"Never," she said firmly. "You should know that by now."

"Hey. Sell to the best or go down in flames like the rest."

Lisa sighed. This was no different from those days when Mike had waited around the corner from school to chase her with squashed worms. "I'd appreciate it if you would keep your spy at home from now on. If you want to know what we're up to, why don't you come on over and see for yourself?"

"A spy, you say? Why, Lisa, what a good idea."

He was hopeless. "Goodbye, snake."

"I love you too, Lisa. Isn't this fun? I'm so glad you came back to town."

She replaced the receiver with care, fighting the urge to slam it down, and sank slowly back into the depths of the big old leather chair. She had a feeling she was only beginning to understand what it was like to be a Loring and to hold a family—or at least a business, together. Suddenly, that had become very important to her. Tomorrow she was going to be thirty-five years old. Thirty-five years—a watershed mark. Funny what a difference it made.

It was time to put her house in order. For too long she had been spinning her wheels, and then the world had crashed down around her.

"Family is what it's all about," Grandfather had whispered to her just before he died. "Don't you forget it. We let things fester between us for too long, you and I. Now you'll have to make it on your own."

Lisa sat very still as she thought about his words. Family. For so many years she had thought it unimportant. And now, she had no one. Not a single relative left in the world. The thought sent a spike of panic through her.

Three raps sounded on her door and she looked up expectantly as Gregory Rice, her store manager, peeked in.

"Busy?" he asked, giving her a friendly smile. Lisa relaxed, smiling back.

"Never too busy for you, Greg. What do you have for me?"

"Only a few reminders." He came in and closed the door, then made his way to the chair on the opposite side of the big oak desk. Tall and slender, Greg had an elegant way of carrying himself. He was one of those men who looked as though clothes had been made expressly to complement his physique.

For just a moment, Lisa thought of the spy Mike had sent over. There was a contrast. While Greg looked like a model for a cologne ad, the spy had worn a suit the way a prizefighter might for a night on the town. Right now, she found Greg's style less threatening.

She couldn't have taken over so smoothly without Greg's input. He'd worked for her grandfather for years, and lately had pretty much run the place by himself. She sometimes wondered if he resented her coming back and taking over after all his hard work. If so, there was no sign of discontent that she could see. And he had certainly been helpful. Still, he had an air of waiting about him, as though he thought there was still another shoe to drop.

Greg sat down and cleared his throat. "Don't forget that the consultant from the bank will be coming over tomorrow to begin research on our situation."

Lisa winced. "Ouch. I had forgotten." She leaned back in the chair and groaned. "I really don't see how some stranger is going to figure out a way to fix what ails us here. I think it's going to have to come from us ourselves."

Greg looked momentarily weary, as though this were an argument he had heard once too often, but he hid it with a cough behind his elegantly manicured hand. "The bank holds our loan, and they call the tune. In order to get the refinancing we've applied for, they insist we submit to some new ideas. Surely that can't hurt."

"Maybe not. But I keep wondering what Grandfather would have said."

Greg laughed shortly. "That's easy. He would have told them all to go to hell, and they would have backed down. But we're living in a new age, Lisa. We've got to keep up with the times."

Greg was right, of course. And she relied on him totally.

"You'll need his help, Lisa Marie," her grandfather had told her just before the end, struggling painfully for the strength to talk. "It's a hard world and retailing is changing every day. He knows the town, he knows the store and my way of doing things. He was here while you were gone. You need him."

He was here while you were gone. Well, Grandfather had always known how to push her guilt buttons. But she had come back to San Feliz determined to make up for lost time in every way, determined not to react negatively to everything her grandfather said, as she always had in the past. He was old and wise and he loved her. She still couldn't understand why it had taken her so long to come to terms with that. But now that she was back, she was going to do it right this time.

"Oh, Greg," she asked as he prepared to leave, "what is the name of the bank representative I'm to see tomorrow?"

"Carson James." Greg hesitated. "No one has told you about him?"

She looked at him blankly. "No. Why?"

"Well..." Greg looked flustered, obviously out of his depth here. "I don't know. They say he's a bit of a playboy." He blinked at her earnestly. "If you like, I'll stick around tomorrow and..."

"Protect me?" She grinned. "Thanks, Greg. I appreciate the offer. But I think I can handle playboys." A picture of the spy she'd confronted popped into her head, but she shook it away as Greg left the office.

"Carson James," Lisa murmured, as she turned to stare at the portrait of her grandfather. She nodded, her face almost grim. "Well, we'll just see what Mr. James has to offer, won't we?"

Carson sat at his desk and stared out at the whitecaps on the ocean. There was quite a view from the seventh floor. Sometimes it seemed like you could see forever—dolphins, pelicans, surfers and sailboats...and the tramp steamers heading for exotic ports. The scene made him want to get up and go.

"Hey, Carson." His supervisor, Ben Capalletti, stopped and looked in, waving an envelope, his warm, kind eyes bright with welcome. "This letter came for you a couple of days ago. You've been gone so much lately, I forgot to give it to you."

Carson took the letter, knowing it would be postmarked Leavenworth. He glanced quickly into Ben's eyes and saw the question mark there. Ben had noticed the postmark. Ben had heard the rumors.

"Thanks," Carson said shortly. He wanted to turn away and crush the envelope in his hand, but his gaze met Ben's and it was no use. Try as he might to keep his distance from the man, that overwhelming warmth just kept breaking down barriers.

Carson's shoulders loosened as though a weight had been taken off them. "Hey," he said, smiling back at the big bear of a man. "How was that driving test? Did Holly pass?"

Given an opportunity, Ben launched into a lengthy and very amusing description of the trials and tribulations of teaching his sixteen-year-old daughter how to drive. Carson laughed often during the telling. Ben always made family life sound like fun. Carson had no doubt he made up half the things he recited, but they made for good stories, so what the heck. And he had to admit, Ben had a bunch of great kids. Why he had felt the need to have so many was a puzzle. Carson had a sudden image of the six of them clustering around Ben like baby birds, mouths opening and closing in anxious supplication, and he bit back the smile the picture conjured up.

"In other words," he said at last as Ben turned to go, "Holly is not yet a free woman of the road."

"No. Thank God. We go again in two weeks to see if she can parallel-park. In the meantime, I'm hiding the car two blocks away from the house so she can't find it to practice with. With any luck, we can keep her from getting her license until she graduates from college. By then at least she ought to have a little more sense.''

Carson laughed, knowing Ben was kidding, and waved as his friend and supervisor left and turned toward his own office. But his smile faded as he looked back down at the envelope in his hand. He'd had three of them now in the four months since his father had tracked him down to this company. And that was still another reason it was time to move on. Shoving it into his pocket, he began to gather up the things he wanted to take home with him.

He was tired, bone weary, and the headache was bouncing around in his head like a basketball. He had been working too hard for months. And for what? The other men in the office put up with this grind for a livelihood to support their families. What the hell was he doing it for? He could do as well fishing off the reef in Tahiti. It was stupid of him to knock himself out this way when he didn't have to. Grabbing his heavy briefcase, he started out, stopping by Capalletti's office to look in.

''You got the file on Covington Electronics?''

Ben nodded. ''Looks like another great job, Carson,'' he said calmly.

Carson nodded. He knew it was. ''I've got Loring's Department Store next.''

''Old man Loring's place. That'll be a tough one.''

Carson thought of Lisa, the demented woman he had met that afternoon. Despite everything, he felt a prickle of anticipation at the thought of seeing her again, as he inevitably would, working with Loring's. Funny. He didn't usually go for the loony ones. ''Right. I'll handle it. Don't worry.''

''You always do.'' Ben smiled at the younger man. ''You'll be dealing with the Loring granddaughter. I guess you've been briefed?''

"Yes." He didn't look forward to dealing with an heir who didn't have any idea of what was going on. No doubt she would be full of opinions and advice, none of it relevant to anything. "Just how young is this little lady?"

"Oh, not as young as you might think. It's been a good ten years or more since she graduated from college."

"Married?"

"Nope. No husband to complicate negotiations. That's one good thing." Ben's face changed thoughtfully. "You've been with us for over a year now, Carson. It's about time we started discussing promotional opportunities, don't you think?"

Carson coughed. This was a point that always made him uncomfortable. Much as he liked working for Ben and liked the job, he couldn't promise to be around long enough to make a promotion worthwhile. "Sure, Ben," he said with an evasive smile. "One of these days. Right now I want to keep my focus on Loring's. Once I get that cleared up, we'll talk."

He knew from the puzzled look on Ben's face that he was fooling no one, but what else could he do? Waving, he started off down the hall toward the elevators. A picture on the wall caught his eye. Palm trees. A turquoise lagoon. His shoulders began to relax and suddenly his headache was gone. It had to be a sign.

Three

"Happy Birthday to me," Lisa sang under her breath as she negotiated the long curve into the underground parking area beneath the department store the next morning. "Happy Birthday to me." She pulled into a parking spot and shut off the engine. "Happy Birthday, dear Lisa." Pulling out the keys, she dropped them into her bag and opened the car door. "Happy Birthday to me."

It was a gorgeous day. She ought to be celebrating at the beach. She ought to have a carful of friends and be speeding toward the ocean with the top down and everyone laughing and calling out to passersby; or planning a big blowout at some fancy, hip downtown club as she had the year before in New York. Friends. Balloons. Loud music. Lots of presents.

"No," she whispered, closing the car door firmly. That was what she might have wanted in the past. But not any longer. This was her thirty-fifth birthday. That was a certain milestone in the life of an unmarried woman. What she really wanted was to celebrate with someone close. Someone who understood. Someone... someone she loved.

"A little late for that," she muttered to herself, listening to the satisfying click of her heels on the concrete floor. Unless she could be quick about it and fall in love by nightfall.

"Not likely," she admitted to the control panel of the elevator as she glided up to the top floor of the building. After all, that crazy thing called love had eluded her for thirty-five years now. Finding it at all appeared to be a long shot. Finding it today would take a miracle.

But something nice would happen today. It had to. It was her birthday.

She stepped off the elevator and almost ran into Garrison Page, a young woman who had worked in billing and came in—almost daily, it seemed to Lisa—to show off her new baby.

"Oh, hi, Miss Loring," Garrison said with a carefree grin. She was dressed in shorts and sandals, with brown hair streaming out around her bare shoulders. "Have you seen my Becky?"

She held the baby up and it squinted its tiny eyes at Lisa. Lisa melted. Babies seemed to do that to her these days.

"What a darling. May I... may I hold her?"

"Sure." Garrison plopped the baby into Lisa's arms and smiled happily. "She's the best baby. If I could get a guarantee that they would all be this good, I'd probably have a dozen of 'em."

Lisa let her briefcase slide to the floor as she took the tiny bundle into her arms and held it close. It felt so soft, smelled so fresh, like powder and daisies and sunshine on a sheet on the clothesline.

Funny, but for years, she'd never noticed babies. She really didn't know the first thing about them. But lately, her world seemed to have been invaded by tiny tots. When she went out, she saw them on every corner. On television, everything was baby food and diapers and toys. They were in restaurants, on the bus, standing on street corners. Why hadn't she ever noticed how many of them there were?

"Do you have any children, Miss Loring?" the young woman asked, watching Lisa's bemused look as she gazed down at Becky.

Lisa managed a smile, but just barely. "No, Garrison. I've never been married."

"Well, that could put a cramp in your style," Garrison said with a laugh. "I don't know how women do it alone. I get all the help in the world. I've got my whole family living with me—my mother and two sisters and a brother-in-law, besides my husband, of course. And everybody pitches in at one time or another."

A big, wonderful ready-made family. Lisa felt a pang of envy. She'd never had one of these. It must be nice to have all that love to fall back on. For just a moment, she felt like telling Garrison it was her birthday. For what reason, she wasn't sure.

"Unless," she scornfully told herself later when she was thinking about it, "you thought she might hand over Becky as a nice birthday present."

At any rate, she held back the information and rather reluctantly gave back the child. "Nice to see you, Garrison. Good luck with Becky."

"Thanks Miss Loring. I'll be coming back to work in a few weeks."

Lisa went on down the hall, holding the smell, the feel and the look of that precious little face in her mind for as long as she could. She found Terry with the phone to her ear, gesturing to her.

"Oh, Miss Loring, Mr. Carson James is on the line."

Mr. James. The bank representative. The day was already off and running.

"I'll take it in my office. Thanks, Terry."

She went on in, lifted the receiver and tried to put a smile in her voice. "Mr. James. I'm looking forward to seeing you. Aren't you scheduled for ten o'clock?"

"I just called to let you know I'm running late. I probably won't make it until about noon. Will that present a problem?"

Lisa frowned. There was something familiar about this voice. "Oh...no, not really. I can have lunch brought in for both of us, if you like, and we can talk right through the noon hour." And it will be my birthday lunch. Don't forget to bring me a present.

"Sure," he said. "That would be great."

Did she know this man? He certainly sounded like someone she had heard before—and recently. "I'm sure you would like to start out with a tour of the store..." she began.

"No, I won't need that," he inserted. "I've already come by a couple of times to get an overview."

"Oh." Well, that was annoying. Without telling her, huh? She couldn't keep a note of sarcasm out of her voice as she went on. "Then I'm sure you know just about everything there is to know about us and are ready to make all sorts of suggestions."

He didn't waste time reacting to her annoyance. "Actually, Miss Loring, I haven't even scratched the surface. Your books are going to tell me what I need to know." He hesitated, then added, "But I do have one little piece of advice, off the cuff, as it were. You know your salesgirl in the Bridal Shoppe? I think her name was Lisa. I don't know what your hiring-and-firing policy is, but I'd advise you to have her tested. The woman's a nut case."

For a long moment, Lisa sat very still, her mind a complete blank. What on earth... Then it came to her like a thunderbolt. This was him. The spy. The spy was no spy. The spy was Carson James, bank person. Oh, my God. And she had accused him...she had told him...she had... Uh-oh. This was going to be some day!

Struggling hard to control her voice, she said, "I'll take that under advisement, Mr. James."

"Right. See you at noon."

She hung up slowly, then she giggled, both hands over her mouth. Oh dear. She *had* made a mistake, hadn't she?

"Fire Lisa on her birthday, will you?" she murmured, half laughing, half in despair. "We'll just see about that, won't we?"

She thought about the man—how he'd looked, how he'd acted—and just the slightest charge of excitement joined her embarrassment. So now he was not a creep she would never see again, not a hired hit man, but a legitimate professional who was supposed to help her. This was definitely going to be interesting.

Her desk contained two messages from Greg. He had gone off to Santa Barbara for the day to get some permit regulations clarified. Note number two said he might be gone all night. She stared at it for a moment, realizing that in the back of her mind she had thought that, once he found out it was her birthday, Greg would get a few people together to help her celebrate. She really knew no one else in town.

"Happy Birthday to me," she muttered, tossing the messages down. But at the same time, she knew it was her own fault. "Oh, well. I'm too big a girl for birthday parties, anyway."

Sinking into her chair, she looked down at her briefcase, still full of financial statements, and at the folder bulging with more figures on her desk. She should get to work. Picking up the phone, she told Terry, "Please hold all my calls for a while." Then she hesitated, wondering if she should tell her secretary that it was her birthday. If she did, everyone in the building would know within minutes. Collections would be formed and someone sent out to buy her a bottle of perfume she would never use. Salesgirls would take their precious lunch hours to run out to pick up a birthday card to present her with. Accountants gathering at the water cooler would take bets on her exact age, and the cafeteria workers would quickly piece together a lopsided cake with Best Wishes written in gluelike frosting. Somehow, she couldn't bear it.

"Thank you, Terry," she said without going into it at all.

She made a call down to Delia in the tearoom and ordered up a gourmet lunch for two—after all, it looked as though this might be her one and only birthday celebration—to be delivered after one. Putting down the phone, she sat back and sighed, pulling her huge round glasses from their case and planting them firmly on the bridge of her nose. Birthday or no birthday, there was work to be done.

The next few hours flew by. She divided her time among her computer, the accounting ledgers and a huge volume of records her grandfather had kept since time immemorial. Now and then she glanced up at the portrait of the old man. Was it just her imagination or was his expression beginning to soften a bit? Maybe he was beginning to believe in her, after all.

Suddenly it was past noon. She didn't notice until she heard someone rapping and the door to her office opened to let in a visitor.

"Hello, there," Carson began, looking about the office. "Your secretary's gone and—"

He stopped and stared, quickly taking in the fact that behind the huge glasses was the same woman he had spoken to the day before. The look on his face would have been comical if she hadn't been so embarrassed about the misunderstanding.

"Oh, no," he said bluntly, his brows pulled together in a dark line. "Not you again."

"Mr. James..." She stood, yanking off her glasses and threw him a wavering smile. Her head was still whirling with the facts and figures she'd been working on. It was going to take her a minute to shift gears.

"Uh-uh," he responded, shaking his head and backing toward the door. "I'm here to talk to Miss Loring."

"Well..." She tried a pleasant smile to calm him. "You see, that's just the problem. I... I am Lisa Loring."

He hesitated and his blue eyes narrowed, assessing the situation. "You run this department store?" he asked, disbelief evident in his tone.

Surely it wasn't *that* hard to believe. She stood a little taller and raised her chin. "Yes, I'm afraid I do."

Warily, he came back into the room. His charcoal-black suit fit perfectly across his wide shoulders, and the crisp white collar of his shirt emphasized his tan. He looked very professional. So why did she imagine she caught a hint of something untamed in his eyes?

"You were acting very weird yesterday," he reminded her, looking her over assessingly.

She nodded, trying not to remember that absurd scene. Overwork. That was what had caused it. Momentary paranoia fed by lack of recreation and rest. She was going to have to toughen herself up.

"I know," she responded quickly. "I'm sorry about that. I thought you were—" she smiled disarmingly "—someone else."

Well, that might account for it. He studied her for a moment. She was just as beautiful as he had remembered. It certainly wouldn't hurt to give her the benefit of the doubt. He shrugged and stepped forward, offering her his hand.

"Carson James," he said out of one corner of his mouth. "Central Coast Bank."

She reached out and took his large, hard hand in her small, slim one. "Lisa Loring," she told him again, just to make sure he believe it. "I'm glad you've come. Won't you please have a seat?"

He sat down, watching her carefully. "Don't worry," she said, slipping back into her grandfather's big old chair, glad for the feeling of security it gave her. Smiling brightly, she looked at him again. So this was the playboy. Yes, she could see evidence of a wandering eye. But she wasn't sure why she had remembered him as being so attractive. His face was hard and tanned, his blue eyes shadowed and wary. Dark hair grew low on his forehead and long on his neck, and his eyebrows were thick and dark, as well. No, he was no Robert Redford. Why had he piqued her interest the day before? She wasn't sure.

"Everything's under control," she continued, still reassuring him. "I know who you really are."

He nodded and began to relax. This might not be so bad, after all. There was no denying that she was very good to look at. She was medium height and slender, and there was a softness to her profile, like that of a porcelain figure. She gave the impression of being a woman whose true colors were pastels, even though the blouse she wore was white and the skirt navy blue.

How old? he wondered. Thirty, maybe. He glanced at her hand for evidence of a wedding ring, and then remembered that Ben had said she was unmarried. Divorced? Maybe. There were no pictures of babies on her desk. A career woman? Possibly. And yet there was that softness about her that made him doubt it. He'd known his share of women who lived for their jobs, and though they often were gorgeous and completely feminine, there was usually a steel-sharp edge to their look, a confidence in their gaze that he didn't see here. She was all businesswoman. But she wasn't driven.

"You're not going to accuse me of being a spy?" he asked, just to make sure.

Her smile was quick but fleeting. "Sorry about that. You see, Mike Kramer has been known to try just about anything, and when I saw you writing into that notebook and talking into your recorder..."

He nodded, and she noticed the cool gleam of intelligence in his crystal-blue eyes. He was bright, anyway. Who knew? She still had him pegged as a playboy, but that didn't mean he didn't know his business. Maybe he would be able to think of a way to save the store.

"Mike Kramer, huh?" he said thoughtfully. He knew Mike. And knowing Mike, he understood her suspicions. Mike was the sort of guy who spiked the punch at the church social and hung the counselor's underwear from the flagpole at scout camp. Mike could be great fun at a ball game or when grabbing a beer with the fellas, but a real pain in everyday life.

"He is your main competitor, isn't he?"

"Yes, he is. Around here, at any rate. Customers can drive down to the malls in Santa Barbara for the large chain stores, but here in San Feliz, it's just Kramer's and Loring's. Always has been." Always will be. But she couldn't say that with any certainty, could she?

He nodded, pulling out a notebook. "What's the rest of your competition like? The boutiques on Shoreline?"

Lisa smiled. At least he seemed to have some idea of what was going on here. Maybe there was hope, after all.

"Yes, I would say so, though we haven't done any sort of definitive market study."

He opened his notebook and took out a pen. "Give me a rough estimate. How much would you say you lost to them in any given week—say, in women's retail?"

"Uh...just a minute." She began to sift through the papers that had so quickly formed amazingly deep piles on her desk in just one morning of work. She had those figures somewhere....

He watched from under his dark eyebrows. What had he been told about her in his original briefing on this job? She was supposed to have had some experience in Europe and years at a big store in New York. But he would bet none of her experience was in the very top position. This was new to her.

He glanced around the room. "Listen, will your assistant, Gregory Rice, be joining us?" he asked. Lisa Loring was manager because her grandfather had left her the business, but he'd been told Rice was the man to see. "I understand he's been with the store for years and has special insight."

She looked up from her search and met his gaze, reading the impatience in his eyes. So it was still "Fire Lisa," was it?

"Don't worry, Mr. James," she replied softly. "I can handle this. I'm just a little distracted at the moment."

She decided to let him try to figure that one out for himself, and went on with her search. But she was beginning to remember what she'd seen in him the day before. It was the masculinity that mattered. When he looked at her, she felt a sense of herself that seemed to translate directly from his gaze. He was Man with a capital *M,* and when his eyes were studying her, she felt that she was Woman—as though her face was meant to be appreciated by a man, her hair was meant to create sensuality, her curves were meant to entice. She almost found herself moving slowly, more gracefully, as though fulfilling some role he put her in.

And those blue eyes . . .

Mentally, she shook herself. There was no time for that. She had business to attend to. She glanced up and found him watching her. The light from behind his head was causing his thick dark lashes to make long shadows on his cheeks. She blinked, caught by the picture he made, then quickly looked back down at the papers she was going through.

She supposed she should be grateful. Hadn't she asked for a man for her birthday? This was most certainly a man. But, as luck would have it, he was the wrong variety. He'd have to be returned.

The corners of her mouth quivered as she held back her smile. What would they say at the exchange counter?

"Can I turn this one in for another?"

"In what way was he defective?"

"There's not a thing wrong with him, believe me. I just need one that's more the marrying kind."

"Oh. Sorry. We're all out of those."

She made a face. Even her fantasies were giving her trouble today.

Carson had watched the last few expressions cross her face, and he was beginning to wonder if she were taking this seriously enough. "You do realize this business is in big trouble, don't you?" he said evenly. "The only way you are going to save it is to cut back—way back."

She didn't look up again, but she countered with the sentence she had used too often lately—the phrase that was most likely to drive Greg wild: "Pinching pennies doesn't attract customers."

Unlike Greg, Carson was ready with a quelling response. "Neither do empty store shelves. And that is what you'll have if you don't have the funds to cover your orders."

She looked up. "Touché," she remarked with a quick smile that disappeared again as she returned to her search.

He felt a small awakening of satisfaction. At least she could disagree without taking everything he said personally. He liked that in a woman—and hadn't found it very often.

His gaze strayed from the elegant curve of her hairline to where an errant wisp of silver-blond hair was curling down along her neck. And from there it was a quick trip to the opening of her silk blouse and the full, rounded swelling of her breasts beneath the fabric. Nice. Very, very nice.

It had been quite some time since he'd been involved with anyone. Lately he'd been wrapped up in his work, and the social side of his life had suffered. Seeing Lisa Loring looking so lovely made him remember what he was missing. The memories stirred feelings he hadn't experienced for a while.

Still, he had to remind himself that this was no time to get involved with a woman. He was about to leave town. But there was no way to turn off the natural reactions he was experiencing. She pleased him—her looks, her manner, her poise. He couldn't help that, could he?

Maybe not. But he knew he would have to curb it—at least until their business was completed. Pulling his gaze away from her, he leaned back in the chair and wrote a few totally meaningless figures in his notebook, just to force back his concentration.

Lisa watched him. She'd found the paper she'd been looking for, and now she was waiting for his attention. "Ready?" she asked at last. His head shot up and his eyes widened slightly. She could tell he hadn't expected her to find that paper—ever. So she smiled.

"If you'd like a moment to prepare for this," she offered with a kindness that was only slightly mocking, "I can wait."

"Uh . . . no, not at all." He straightened in his chair and poised his pen over the notebook. He surveyed her coolly. She seemed almost too perceptive for her own good. A man would have to stay on his toes with this one. "Shoot."

Nodding, she settled back in her chair and replaced her glasses. Crossing her legs, she read from the paper, stopping to make comments on some of the figures as she recited them, totally engrossed in work again. He followed along, responding, jotting down notes, asking questions that she invariably answered intelligently.

His first impression was fading away rapidly. This woman was as sharp a businessperson as any he had ever dealt with before, male or female. In fact, this woman was probably the most fascinating businessperson he had ever met.

There was a softness, a femininity to her—the kind of thing that made a man wonder what she would feel like in his arms. And then she plunked those glasses on her nose and straightened her shoulders and it was as though she'd suddenly developed spines to make sure that kind of thing didn't happen. "Touch me not," her body language said loud and clear. That was probably a clue to why her ring finger looked so naked. She was probably as much a workaholic as he had been lately. Too bad.

"Do you have the list of suppliers in that stack?" she asked, and her eyes met his for just a moment. There was a jolt there, just a tiny flash of sensual identification, and he had to repress a smile. He handed her the list she'd asked for but he didn't say a word. A thought had just struck him—maybe it was her big dark eyes that were bothering him so much. Feminine dark eyes seemed to be a thing with him lately. He ought to watch that.

The big, dark eyes of Michi Ann Nakashima had led him astray two days in a row, now. She'd been at his door first thing this morning, requesting more instant gallantry. He glanced down at the new scratches on his left hand and grimaced. Today the ginger cat had worked its way under the house next door, and somehow he had found himself recruited to climb under and drag it out.

"He knows you now, mister," Michi had said so earnestly. "I know he won't scratch you this time."

Right. And the check is in the mail. When would he ever learn?

Wincing, he picked up a pile of accounting papers and a slick brochure fell out from between the pages. Catching it before it hit the floor, he turned to the front cover to see what it was and where it belonged.

But this brochure had nothing to do with business, and was not even put out by Loring's. It was a catalog from a baby-furniture company. A lovely white crib was marked with a large circle in ink. Somehow he didn't think she was planning to order it to fill out the Loring's baby line.

He glanced at her, but she was hard at work creating a spreadsheet on her computer monitor, her lower lip caught between her teeth, all attention on the screen. He looked back down at the crib. Unmarried, Ben had told him. Maybe it was a present for a sister or something.

"You know what?" Lisa said suddenly, throwing down her pencil and swinging toward him on her chair. "We're going to need the annual reports from ten years back and they're down in the storeroom." Reaching for the phone, she dialed a number and waited for an answer. "They're out to lunch," she concluded, giving up and putting back the receiver. "You want to go down with me and dig them up for ourselves?"

The idea had its appeal. His restless soul was being particularly troublesome today. Moving around would help.

"Lead on," he said, as he rose from his chair. He opened the door and held it for her, wondering if she realized his politeness was mostly a ruse to get her to pass close by so he could catch the scent of her hair.

Her eyes met his just as she passed him, and he knew in that one flashing moment that not much went over her head. She knew. And her look, with the smile turned down on one side, told him he was chasing butterflies. She had no intention of playing any sort of game.

He let the door close with a twisted grin on his own lips. It had been a long time since he'd met a woman who was as quick to pick up the nuances as this one. Yes, she definitely intrigued him.

Four

The storeroom was a cavernous space in the basement holding personal property rather than retail supplies. Eighty years of history were littered about the room.

"What's down here?" Carson asked, following Lisa as she threaded her way through the jumbled items that loomed mysteriously in the gloomy interior.

"All kinds of stuff. Things my grandfather couldn't bear to part with." She pointed toward two huge golden spires peeking up above a dustcover. "Parts of old floats from parades twenty years ago. That was Miss Liberty's crown, I think, for some Fourth of July celebration." She patted a large stuffed giraffe with one ear missing and pointed out a chandelier hanging lopsidedly from the high ceiling. "Items that didn't sell. Product lines that didn't pan out."

She pivoted slowly, taking it all in—all that ancient, dusty glory. How she had loved this place as a child. She'd spent hours down here. It had been her own private playground.

Her fingers trailed a path through a layer of age on the hood of a midget Model T replica and she felt a twinge of regret. Maybe this was where she had first learned to live in dreamland. The imaginary princes and pirates who had once saved her from dragons and renegades—had they all slowly evolved into her tweed-wearing hero, the man she had lately reserved as the only possible father for her children? Was that why he seemed to be just as hard to find in real life as her heroic fantasy figures had been in her younger days?

She turned to catch a glimpse of Carson as he poked his way through the remnants of an old carousel. He was real. He was a man. But try as she might, she couldn't imagine him in tweed. But gosh, did it have to be tweed? Maybe a nice cardigan... Staring at him, she squinted her eyes and tried to picture him sitting thoughtfully beside a fireplace, a pipe in one hand, a volume of Wordsworth in the other. He turned and caught her glance, his mouth twisting in a sardonic smile, his eyes asking personal questions, and laughter bubbled up her throat as she quickly turned away.

But she regretted it. She didn't want to give him the impression she was interested because, of course, she wasn't.

"Hey!" he called out a moment later. "Look what I found."

He was rummaging around behind an old plastic version of Santa's sleigh and seemed to have come upon a stash of old portraits.

"What are those?" She turned and walked slowly toward him. "I don't think I've ever seen them before." She joined him in a look.

Portraits in gilt frames were stacked like so much cordwood: paintings of her grandfather, her great-grandfather, her grandmother and two of her grandfather's sisters, her father as a very young man, her great-grandmother.

And atop an old upright piano sat a stack of faded, browning photographs of her family. *Her family*. The very concept made her heart race. There was her father in his Navy pilot's uniform, her father graduating from college, her father cutting the ribbon on a new lunchroom in the department store. And then there was a picture of her father and mother, with little Lisa, probably about four years old, straggling at the side, seemingly an onlooker to their relationship.

But Lisa hardly noticed that. She had so few pictures of her mother. And this was one of the best she'd ever seen.

"Wow. Who's the celebrity?" Carson asked, looking over her shoulder.

She smiled quickly. "That's no celebrity. She was my mother."

"She was a very beautiful woman."

Lisa nodded. "She was."

Valerie Hopkins Loring had been the sort of beauty you usually only saw in the movies. There she was, staring out of the picture, laughing, her eyebrows raised in happy surprise, her blond curls tumbling about her face—so gorgeous, and such a flirt.

"A real heartbreaker," Carson observed softly.

Lisa nodded again. She couldn't dispute that. By all accounts, her mother's wedding day had been a time of mourning for half the men in town. Her beautiful mother. The face she felt she hardly knew. She traced the outline of it with her finger and found she had a lump in her throat.

Carson looked at Lisa and wondered, but he didn't ask. He could see that emotion was building in her. And finally she volunteered the information.

"My...my parents were killed in a boating accident in the Caribbean when I was ten," she told him. She turned and looked at him, trying to smile. "Sometimes it just comes back to me so forcefully,'' she said, her voice breaking. And suddenly her eyes were brimming with tears.

He reached for her. There was nothing else he could do. She fit into his arms as though she belonged there, and for just a moment, she melted against him, clinging.

But before he could completely assimilate the sensations that shot through him, she was gone again, pulling back and away and laughing self-consciously.

''I'm sorry.'' She quickly wiped her eyes. Darn it all, what was wrong with her? She had hardly cried over Grandfather's death, and now this. ''This is really silly. I don't usually do this.''

She couldn't imagine where this emotion had come from. She'd grown up slightly embarrassed about her flighty, silly mother. Her grandfather had harbored a lot of resentment toward the woman he believed had ruined his son, and had made no bones about his feelings. For years her mother's memory had been faint to her, a backdrop in her busy life. But since she'd come home, sudden, clear recollections had begun to haunt her and she was beginning to see her mother in a whole new light. She flashed Carson a quick smile. Emotions she didn't know she possessed were throwing her off balance. She had to learn to hide them.

He stood very still, watching her, his arms at his sides, feeling helpless in a deep, scary way he didn't remember ever having felt before. He ached to comfort her, but he knew that wasn't what she wanted, and he held it back. But that feeling he'd had when she was in his arms... What was it? Some kind of protectiveness? As though he would gladly shelter her from the world and die doing it. He flexed his shoulders and tried to shake the remnants off. Strange. Very, very strange.

She turned and began dusting off some less sentimental pictures. He came up beside her and watched her work. "So you grew up without parents?" he asked softly.

She nodded. "Just my grandfather." She glanced up at him as though she sensed something. "And you?"

That was always an awkward question for him. "I...my mother died when I was born. And my father— Well, I grew up with relatives. Cousins. They took me in."

She smiled, her lashes still wet from the tears. "So you're an orphan, too."

He didn't answer. There was no way he was going to try to tell her the truth—that his father was in prison, that his father always seemed to be in one prison or another, and had been ever since he could remember. Embezzlement, fraud, misappropriation of funds, forged checks—whatever they called it, he was a thief, and an expert at getting caught at it. But that was something Carson never told people.

Instead of answering, he countered with another question. "Are you an only child, too?"

She nodded. They smiled at each other for a moment, bound by a close feeling of kinship. She thought of the comforting embrace he'd offered her, and she wanted to do something, say something, to thank him. But somehow the words wouldn't come out right. She didn't want to encourage him. He most certainly wasn't the kind of man she was looking for. She shifted her gaze from his.

"Well, we'd better get those reports," she said. She was the first to turn away. "They're over there, in those file cabinets against the wall, next to that old casting display."

The dust-covered panorama featured two mannequins dressed in hip boots and other fly-fishing regalia, casting their lures into a river made of Styrofoam, all life-size. Carson loved it.

"When was this used?" he asked, going in to touch the line that still extended from the rod and run his finger down to the reel.

She had followed him in, stepping carefully around the ancient Styrofoam. "I remember it from when I was a little girl. I think Grandfather used to bring it out every year at the opening of the season."

"This is great."

She smiled, enjoying his candid pleasure in such a silly thing. He was an attractive man. It was just too bad—

She took a careless step and lost her balance.

"Oh!"

She caught herself against the mannequin and nearly took it over with her. Out of the corner of her eye, she could see Carson approaching, ready to catch her. He would think she had set this up, and that would make the tension that was beginning to percolate between them all the more dangerous. She fought hard for control of her balance and managed to steady the mannequin, depending on it to keep her upright.

"I'm okay," she said quickly.

And then she tried to move her head.

"Uh-oh."

He frowned, coming in closer. "What is it?"

"I, uh..." She reached up and tried to free herself. "I seem to have got my hair caught." Ridiculous. She had a hook in her hair.

"Ouch!"

It snagged her finger. The hook was still lethal, after all these years.

Carson took over without giving her any more room for protest. "Just a minute. Hold very still," he told her, coming close. "You can't get this. I'll have to do it." And he came even closer.

"You know, I can probably get it myself," she ventured without much conviction.

"Don't be such a coward." He smiled down at her. "I haven't lost a patient yet."

Her heart was beginning to pound and that was embarrassing. He had to lean over her to reach the hook. He was going to hear her racing heartbeat. She tried holding her breath, but that only seemed to make it worse.

"Hold still," he repeated softly as he worked on the hook. "Just a minute more."

She closed her eyes so that she wouldn't have to stare at what was only an inch from her face: his crisp hairline and the dark stubble of his beard that was just beginning to emerge. But the warm scent of his body was something she couldn't turn off. She was breathing it in. His body was pressing against hers as he worked, and she felt as though she were about to suffocate.

She'd known this was bound to happen. She'd felt it when he had tried to comfort her a few minutes before. She couldn't take comfort from him. It would turn into something more as fast as it took that thought to surface. And so she had drawn away, in order to protect herself.

But what could she do here? She was stuck. She couldn't have moved if she'd wanted to. So she closed her eyes and endured the heart-stopping excitement his body seemed to magically conjure up in hers. In a moment he would be through, and she would be able to breathe again.

Carson's fingers stilled in her hair. The hook was out, but he didn't want to move. She felt very good right where she was. His coat was hanging open and her full breasts were pressed to his chest. Thinking of them made the hard, washboard muscles of his stomach contract. He left his body where it was and drew back only his head and shoulders, so that he could look down at her.

He'd meant to avoid this sort of thing. Mixing business and romance was always a recipe for disaster. He knew he should shove himself away from her and head for the hills. But he couldn't do it. Not this time. The pull was just too strong.

Her face was tilted up. Her eyes were almost closed, and her lips were slightly parted. Every instinct told him to go for it. Taking a deep breath, he bent to take her mouth with his.

"No."

For just a moment, he wasn't sure if he had really heard her speak. He held back but didn't move away, trembling fractions of an inch from her lips. "No?" he whispered, as though he couldn't quite believe it.

"No." She said it more firmly this time. "No. Don't kiss me."

He stepped back a little farther, but was still close. His hands slipped down to take the lapels of her shirt in his grasp, and he held them lightly. "Why not?" he asked, as though it was nothing but a casual question.

She shook her head slowly, her eyes huge in the dim light. "Because I don't want you to." Her words were clear and concise. She meant every word she said.

Or did she? Carson still hesitated. Sometimes it wasn't easy to decipher what a woman actually meant. He'd been so sure. . . .

"Your eyes weren't saying no," he told her softly.

She sighed and gave a little half-laugh. "I know." She looked at him with regret. "Okay, it's true. Every impulse in my body is dying to have you kiss me."

His blue eyes were clouded with doubt. "Well, then . . ."

She had to make him understand. Bringing her two hands up, she placed them on his chest and gave a slight push to let him know she meant it. "My brain takes precedence over my body any day. And it says no, loud and clear."

He stared at her for a moment, then pulled back, swinging away from her, and watched as she straightened herself and brushed down her clothes.

"What is it? You don't want to get involved with business associates?" he asked, his eyes too dark to read.

She looked at him, feeling relief but also chagrin. "No. It's not that." There was really no percentage in polite lies. She had been through enough of that in her time. She would tell him the truth. He deserved as much.

"I'll level with you, Carson. I'm too old to play around anymore. I know what I need, and playing around has nothing to do with it."

He looked at her, perplexed. Playing around was all there was. Playing around was what made life worthwhile. Didn't she know that? Hadn't she heard?

"Just what is it that you think you need?"

She made her way gingerly out of the display and started toward the file cabinets. He followed close behind.

"That's an easy one," she said as she walked briskly toward her goal. "I need the whole shot. The little cottage where the roses bloom. Two cats in the yard. A swing set out back."

He drew away as though she'd stung him. "And a little white crib in the nursery," he murmured, putting two and two together.

"What?" she questioned, but he shook his head. "Well, you can see what I mean, can't you?" she went on. "What I want is about as diametrically opposed to what you want as you can get. We're incompatible."

They'd reached the cabinets. Pulling out a drawer, she found what she wanted and began to pull out files, handing them to him.

He took them, but the frown still clouded his face. "How do you know what I want?" he asked her.

She laughed softly. "Now *that* I can see in your eyes." She slammed the drawers and they started back through the cavernous room with their arms full of folders.

"Let me get this straight," he said without bothering to dispute her contention about what he wanted. He had a feeling she had it right, anyway. It made him want to laugh. She was so damn honest. "The way I see it, you still believe in fairy tales."

She flashed him a quick smile. "Happy endings? Absolutely." She punched the button for the freight elevator.

"Then if we put this into fairy-tale terms..." he began, humor glistening in his blue eyes.

"You are the Big Bad Wolf," she finished for him, turning to catch his reaction in his eyes, wondering how he was going to take that.

He looked downright shocked. "What? I always thought of myself as the handsome prince."

She laughed as the doors slid open and she walked into the cargo carrier. "Think again."

"No. Come on," he said, following her and looking hurt. "The handsome prince offers the lovely damsel romance...excitement..."

"All of which you can handle, I'm sure." She saw a bit too much agreement in his eyes this time and she turned away, shaking her head. "That's the version they tell on the male side of the hogan, isn't it? It's a little different on the female side. We like to interpret 'They lived happily ever after' as meaning they get married and have a bunch of kids."

The creaking elevator reached its destination. Carson put a hand out to hold the door for her. "What's so happy about that?" he asked archly.

She knew he was goading her, but she wasn't in the mood for righteous indignation. Instead, she began to walk firmly toward her office, knowing he would come along beside her. "Oh, sure. I suppose you think 'happily ever after' means finding another lovely damsel next week."

He didn't answer right away. The office staff was sparse and Terry wasn't at her desk. They took advantage of that to dump the files they were carrying all over her chairs and side table before turning in toward Lisa's office. As they reached the doorway, Carson stopped her, putting a hand up against the doorframe to bar her entry for a moment, forcing her to look up into his face. She was surprised to see that he had been mulling over her last statement all this time.

"Believe it or not," he declared, his eyes clear and slightly angry, "I don't think I'm really that shallow."

She'd gone too far. She wished she could recall her words. "Look, I didn't mean to imply you were...like that. It's just that—"

"What you implied was, you and I can't get to know each other better because you are looking for a husband, and I'm not husband material."

She flushed, wishing they had never gotten into this. "No. What I meant to say was, I'm ready at this stage of my life to get serious, and I don't think you are."

He shrugged. "Same thing. But you don't even know me. You're reacting to an image. You haven't bothered to dig beneath that and get to the truth. Have you?"

He was absolutely right. She leaned back a little, looking him over, trying to get beyond the blue eyes... and the wide shoulders...and the hard, masculine face...and tried to compare him to her tweedy man, the one who would father her children and head her household. For just a moment, she let herself pretend that she might be able to squeeze Carson James into that picture, and just the thought of it made her pulse race again. What if....?

But then her gaze met his and she saw the gleam of humor curling around the smoky sensuality the man couldn't help but exude. Ah, yes. That was the major sticking point. The future father of her children would never look at a woman that provocatively. Unable to stop herself, she started to laugh.

"What?" He was at a loss. Could he really be unaware of how provocative he looked?

"I'm sorry. It's not really you." She laughed again, throwing her hand out as though to ask his forbearance, her fingertips grazing his chest. He reached out and captured her hand, holding her loosely by the wrist.

"I never realized I cut quite such a comical figure," he said, his eyes searching hers.

"No, it's not that. It's just..." And before she realized what she was doing, there went her other hand, sliding along the lapel of his suit coat. It was just too easy to touch him. They were too physical with each other at much too early a stage. They didn't know each other well enough to be feeling so close.

She pulled away and looked at him. They were no longer touching, but her awareness of his physical presence was like a faint throbbing in her body.

"You're a very attractive man, Carson, but you're not what I'm looking for," she stated simply and honestly, wishing that just the saying of it would help to distance them from each other, but knowing that it wasn't enough.

He stared back at her. "Can't we be friends?" he asked softly.

She shook her head slowly, caught by the expression in his crystal-blue eyes. "No," she replied softly. "I don't think we can."

He looked as though her answer pained him. "It wouldn't be for long," he urged. "I'm leaving for Tahiti soon."

"Oh." Well, that was good, wasn't it? He was just what she'd thought—a playboy disguised as a banker. But he was leaving, so she could relax around him. Couldn't she? "Why Tahiti?"

His shrug was open, casual. "Because it's different. And I've never been there."

She stared at him for a moment, then threw her hands up, laughing. "All right, Mr. Carson James. Enough messing with my mind. You just proved that everything I've been saying is absolutely true."

His grin was crooked. "Oh, yeah?"

"Yes. I want stability. You want to take off for faraway places. Just like I said, we are diametrically opposed." She shoved open the door of her office, tossing him a saucy look over her shoulder. "So stop trying to undermine my judgment. I know what I'm doing."

She stopped in her tracks. Her office had been turned into a small, elegant French restaurant. Books and papers had been moved to a table along the back of the room. A lace cloth had been thrown over her desk. Silver serving dishes of rich food gleamed. Candles sat waiting to be lit. Crystal sparkled. China shone.

She'd said a gourmet meal. She supposed Delia had found out who was coming to lunch and drawn her own conclusions. Carson James's reputation was probably widespread. This looked like an invitation to romance if ever she'd seen one. She was going to have to have a talk with that woman.

She glanced at James and saw that he was as flabbergasted as she was. It wouldn't do to let him know she hadn't meant it to turn out quite this way. So she smiled.

"Ah, I see the food is here. Would you like to sit down and eat?"

He didn't say a word. Awestruck, no doubt, she told herself as she watched him take a chair and move it up to the desk. What must he be thinking? Here she claimed to have no interest in him romantically, and then she sprang this on him.

And it was pretty awe-inspiring. Mushrooms sautéed in white wine, artichokes stuffed with tiny bay shrimps, and chicken *moutarde,* with a special torte for dessert. He was probably wondering what on earth could have inspired such an extravagant celebration.

Carson was wondering exactly that. He'd had working lunches before, but never anything like this elaborate display. Did they have food like this in Tahiti?

Never mind. They had tropical fruit in Tahiti, and women who lived for today and weren't setting up housekeeping arrangements. Two cats in the yard—right. He glanced at the scratches covering the backs of his hands and grimaced.

It was a shame, but he was afraid he was going to have to give Miss Lisa Loring a rather wide berth. No matter how much fun he'd had arguing with her at the time, she'd been absolutely right. Their goals were incompatible. He appreciated the way she'd brought that out in the open right away. Now, neither of them had any illusions. They would be able to steer away from trouble because, knowing exactly where they each stood, they would avoid getting involved, despite the obvious natural attraction between the two of them. It was that simple. Forewarned was forearmed.

"Do you like the food?" she asked, her lips tilted in a small smile, once he seemed to have tried everything.

"Of course," he replied, looking wary, as though he weren't sure how he was going to be expected to pay for his supper. "It's fine."

The food was more than fine. It was utterly delicious. He took another bite of chicken and glanced at her from under his dark eyebrows. "If you eat this way every day, no wonder this store is going under," he commented, watching her reaction.

She smiled. "I don't eat this way every day."

The way she said it made him sure there was more to this than met the eye. "Then why today?" he probed. "Is there some special reason?"

She shook her head, the smile still shining in her eyes. "There is a reason. But it's a secret."

"A secret." His head tilted to the side as he searched her eyes for clues. "What kind of secret?"

She folded her hands and stared right back. "The kind you don't tell anyone."

"Oh, no." He shook his head decisively. "You always have to tell one person."

"Do you?"

"Sure. Otherwise it doesn't even count as a secret. It's like the old puzzle about the tree—if it falls in the forest and there is no one there to hear it, does it make any noise?"

"Does it?"

"How should I know? I wasn't there at the time." His smile was long and lazy. "But I'm here. And you can tell me your secret."

She liked it when he grinned that way. Why had she told him they couldn't be friends? What a grouch she was turning into. A little friendliness couldn't hurt. He was going to Tahiti.

"I see," she said. "So what are you? The designated secret person?"

"That's me."

She thought for a moment, studying the weave of the fabric of his sleeve. If she told him, he would be the only person on the West Coast who knew. She wasn't sure why that made her skin prickle, but it did. Still, she was going to tell him. For some crazy reason, she *wanted* him to be the only one who knew.

"Okay," she agreed at last.

He waited.

"You understand about secrets, don't you?" she asked him. She was half serious, half teasing, and he knew it. "I mean, if I tell you, you won't tell anyone else."

He held up his hand. "Scout's honor."

"You and I will be the only ones who know."

He nodded, waiting, finding that concept somehow very pleasing.

She hesitated. "Okay." She looked directly into his eyes. "Here it is—this day... today... it's my birthday."

"Your birthday?" He'd never been big on such occasions himself, but he knew women usually found them very important. And here she was, having her birthday lunch with him—a man she didn't even know. Even to him it seemed a little sad. "And nobody knows?"

She nodded. "I've only been back for a few weeks," she explained. "I've had cards and phone calls from friends in New York. But there's no one here..." Her voice trailed off, as though she suddenly realized the poignancy of it all herself.

Carson stared at her hair. It was beginning to pull away from the neat pins that had held it in place. The incident with the fishing lure hadn't helped maintain her bun. But now it was giving up, calling it a day, letting hair be hair, and it shimmered around her face like a soft halo.

"What are you doing tonight?" he asked on impulse. "Let's go dancing."

She didn't look at him. Instead, she began to stack the dishes. "We decided not to date. Remember?"

"No. *You* decided. But this won't be a real date. Someone's got to take you out for your birthday."

Looking up, she studied his face, looking for the punch line. Surely he was joking. "Thanks, but no thanks," she said. "I've got work to do." She rose and placed the dishes on a tray by the door.

He saw the wariness in her, the reluctance to risk letting someone close. He recognized it immediately, because he lived with it every day. They had so much in common. And yet they were so very different in so many ways. She was trying hard to be tough, to be strong. But to him she just looked slender and vulnerable. And those qualities were awakening responses in him that should probably be left alone.

But it was okay. They both knew where they stood and they wouldn't let things get out of hand.

She slid back into her chair and reached for her glasses. "I guess we'd better get back to work," she announced crisply, swiveling in her seat to face the computer monitor again.

He rose and went out to retrieve some of the folders from the huge pile they had brought up from the basement. Terry was back at her desk and she gave him one of those female smiles of appreciative welcome he was used to. That made him feel a little better. He went back in and looked at Lisa. When she glanced up at him through the thick reading glasses, he might have been a couch for all the notice she paid.

"Tell me what you know about returns policies at other stores in the area," she said. "I don't like the way we've been handling it here. I'd like to make some changes."

He sat down and nodded. Well, he thought, slouching in his chair, whatever else, she was determined to take over Loring's and do a good job of it. That was clear enough. What was not clear was just exactly how she was going to do it when everything was stacked against her.

Carson hesitated. The way he saw it, he had only two good options. First, he could tell her the truth and advise her to get out while the getting was good, cutting her losses. That wasn't exactly what he had been sent to do, but it would actually be the kindest thing in the long run. On the other hand, he could pitch in and help her fight. That would take them down a long and painful path, and might end up exactly where the first option did anyway.

"I'll have to look into returns policies," he told her. "I'll get back to you on it."

She nodded, not looking up, and as she bent her head over an accounting ledger, he watched the way she caught her lower lip with her teeth as she concentrated on the column of figures she was adding up. Yesterday he had thought she was demented. Today he was seeing a totally different woman.

"Tell me something," he asked suddenly, interrupting the flow of her work. "What do you really think of this place?"

She raised her gaze and stared at him. "What do you mean?"

"Loring's was your grandfather's life. But you left years ago. It can't be yours. Just how much emotional energy do you have to invest in this? Do you love this place? Or is this just another job to you?"

She was quiet for a long moment. "There was a sort of rift between my grandfather and me for a number of years," she replied at last, not meeting his gaze. "I had to prove something to him before I could come back."

"So now, who are you trying to prove something to?"

She looked up and favored him with a smile that came and went very quickly. "Myself."

He nodded slowly. "I'll tell you straight out. This place is a dump."

Color rushed into her cheeks. She felt as though an ancestor or a sibling were being attacked.

"Now don't get mad," he hurried to say. "Let me finish. I'd like you to look at it objectively. This place was once the epitome of everything a small-town department store should be. But that was years ago. When your grandfather got old, he let this place get old. Loring's as it stands right now is hardly worth saving." Leaning forward, he looked for answers in her eyes. "What I want to know is— is there a soul to this business? Is there something here that I should care about saving?"

Lisa was very still for a long moment. For some ridiculous reason, she was trembling just a little. She only wished she had the right words to say to Carson. He was waiting, his blue eyes deep as midnight, and she could tell a lot was going to hinge upon her answer.

"I'm not sure how to answer that," she said at last, feeling like a failure. "I'm not sure I have an answer."

He closed his book with a snap. "Then I don't know why we should bother going on."

Her heart fell. She wanted to reach for him, take hold of his arm. "You can't give up on me just like that."

He leaned closer once again, looking deep into her eyes. "I'm not giving up on you, Lisa," he told her softly. "I'm asking that you not give up on you. I want you to take some time to reach down inside yourself and find out what you really want here. Is this business still driven by your grandfather and his plans? Or have you really taken over?''

He rose and touched her cheek with a careless finger, surprising her again. ''I'll tell you what I want you to do, Lisa. I want you to tear yourself away from these books and go out on the beach and stare into the waves and think. Just think. Let yourself feel. Let yourself float. And get in touch with what it is you really want, and why you want it.''

Lisa rose too, her knees shaking, and she wasn't really sure why. She felt defensive about Loring's, defensive about her emotional investment; and yet she couldn't put into words anything that she felt. So she just reacted.

''That's hogwash and you know it! It's perfectly clear what we have to do. If you can't help me, maybe the bank had better send over someone else.''

He smiled at her, shaking his head, letting her anger slide off him like the breeze. ''Are you staying in that big old place of your grandfather's on the beach?'' he interjected.

She paused. ''Yes, but—''

''I'll come by tonight,'' he promised, heading for the office door. ''I hope you know the answer by then.'' He stopped halfway through the doorway and glanced back, as if already looking forward to seeing her later. But it was okay. They were incompatible. And he was leaving soon. Everything would be okay.

He consulted his watch. ''I'm going down to the marina and do a little sailing.'' His look was mischievous. ''Gotta practice up for Tahiti.''

She almost laughed, more in despair than humor. ''No doubt.''

And then, with a jaunty wave, he was gone.

She pulled her glasses off and absently played with them. Carson James. He would have been a gift from heaven if she were younger. But she couldn't waste her time and energy on someone like him. It was far too late in the game.

But for a moment she couldn't help imagining what it would be like to take a man like Carson, with all the qualities that made him so attractive, and add the things she needed, change him into someone so special.…

But that was crazy. Why would she want to do something like that? She didn't want to change Carson. She wanted to find someone who was already what she needed. That was the only way. Carson James was completely out of the question. She needed a family man. As a future father for her children, he was impossible. As a lover, however… She shivered just thinking about it, and had to laugh at herself. It had been much too long since she'd had a man in her life. With a melancholy sigh, she turned back to her books.

Five

Lisa parked her car in the drive and sat staring at the big old Victorian monstrosity she now called home.

Home, sweet home. Home was where the heart was.

"Home is where," Lisa murmured, trying to remember the correct wording, "when you have nowhere else to go, they have to take you in." Who had said that? Someone horribly cynical.

She left the car and walked around to the front of the house, shading her eyes to look out at the sunset that was streaking salmon across a sky as silver as the ocean. A salty breeze teased her hair. The concrete sidewalk beneath her feet was covered with sand that crunched beneath the hard leather soles of her pumps.

Okay. She'd gazed into the waves, now where was her revelation? "I want to save Loring's," she said aloud to the wind. "I want to save Loring's because it is my way of validating what my family has always been and stood for."

Nice words. But what did they really mean? Carson would see through a fraud like that in a minute. Sighing, she turned to go into the house and bumped into something on wheels that had been left practically on her doorstep.

It was light, made of aluminum. She caught hold of it before it overturned and looked it over. A baby buggy. Well, not exactly, more like a doll's buggy, with a little mattress and a pink pillow. Some little girl must have been playing with it on the beach and left it behind when she went home. All kinds of things were always being left in Lisa's front yard—inner tubes, beach towels, volleyballs. And now a baby buggy.

Lisa set the buggy up next to the sidewalk so the little girl could find it easily when she came back for it, as surely she would. A yellow cardboard plaque fluttered from the handle. Baby Aboard it stated rather forlornly.

Lisa smiled and turned to pick up her mail from the box. Birthday cards, bills, advertisements—she threw them all on the table in the living room and went on into the kitchen to fix herself a snack. She had so much work to do, there really wasn't time for a real meal.

"But wait," something screamed inside her. "It's your birthday!"

Turning slowly, she looked at the clock on the wall. "Maybe I could just take one hour..."

Her gaze flashed toward the bureau drawer where her guilty secret was hidden and she let her breath out slowly. She didn't smoke. She didn't drink, except a sip or two to be sociable. She didn't have any sort of love life—unfortunately. She didn't even binge on chocolate truffles. But she did have a vice—a special, secret thing she loved to do that no one else knew about.

She hardly ever let herself go long enough to indulge in it. But tonight seemed the perfect time. "Just one hour," she promised as she pulled out the bureau drawer and extracted a handful of glossy magazines. "I'll even set the alarm."

She carried her treasure to the most comfortable couch in the den and flopped down, kicking off her shoes, sighing with contentment. Spreading the magazines out on her lap, she stared at them. Baby Talk was the logo above the picture of a fat, laughing toddler on one of them. Growing Up Right said another. Smiling with anticipation, she slipped on her glasses and began to flip slowly through the pages, savoring every picture, devouring every article. Who would have dreamed there was so much to know about these little chubby-cheeked creatures?

And she had found, in recent weeks, that she had an insatiable need to know it all. Her mind was on saving Loring's, but her heart was tangled up in baby blankets. She wanted a child.

Then why weren't you working for that all these years? she asked herself severely. You certainly haven't done a thing to advance this supposed goal of yours.

It was true. She hadn't even tried to attract marriage. In fact, she had shoved it away on numerous occasions. And it wasn't as though she had really been deprived of options up to now. All in all, she had done exactly what she wanted to. Was that a crime? She'd made her choices and taken the consequences. Up to now, that had been fine. But suddenly everything had changed.

Marriage. Babies. Thirty-five.

The words swirled through her head. It wasn't fair. If she were a man, there would still be so much time. But because she was a woman, she was faced with the fact that there was no more time left. It was practically now or never. And what was she going to do about it?

Look at magazines. Not very productive, but at least it comforted her for the short run.

Time passed unnoticed. At one point she settled back and pulled her legs up under her skirt. Later, she absently pulled the pins out of her hair and let it fall naturally about her shoulders, lost the whole time in the unfamiliar world of nutritional comparisons on formulas and the relative merits of cloth versus paper diapers. Was it best to start solids before the first smile? How about swimming lessons before the first step?

She was shuddering over the reported horrors of croup when a creaking sound made her jump and turn. Carson James stood in the doorway of the room.

"Hi," he said pleasantly, as though he always arrived this way, as though they were old friends and easy together. "I knocked, but no one answered. I came around the side and I could see you reading here on the couch, so I came in through the French doors from the patio."

She swallowed and nodded, slipping the magazines together into one compact pile and looking out of the corner of her eye for someplace to hide them. "Uh . . . hi," she responded weakly.

He entered the room and flopped down into an easy chair across from her. "Not very secure around here, you know. You ought to work on that."

"True." She was trying to shove the baby magazines under a cushion. Why did they embarrass her? She wasn't sure; she just knew they did.

"I see you're hard at work," he remarked casually. "What are those? Financial reports?"

"Not exactly." They didn't fit under the cushion. A cover photo of two chubby legs protruded from beneath the brocade. She stared at them. So did Carson.

"What is that?" Reaching with his long arm, he pulled it out and held it dangling from his fingertips as though it were a dirty diaper. He stared at the magazine, digesting its identity, taking in its significance and regretting it—all at once.

"Oh," he said faintly. "Baby stuff."

"You know that birthday I had today?" she broke in quickly. "I turned thirty-five. Thirty-five years old."

She stopped and looked at him expectantly, as though that must surely explain the situation. Was she really going to have to describe to him exactly how much she yearned for motherhood? She hoped not. He was a bright guy. Surely he would figure it out on his own and she wouldn't have to go into detail. But he was staring at her, obviously waiting to hear the rest.

"So?" he responded at last when it looked as though she were finished, after all. He shrugged. "I was thirty-five a few years ago. And look, everything still works just fine."

"I know, but you're a man."

"True." Despite all his willpower, his eyes darkened as he looked at her. "And you're a woman. I'd noticed that."

She shook her head, still trying to get through to him on the calm level of logic without going into explicit detail. "We have different biological functions," she said vaguely.

"No kidding?" He sat back and watched her levelly. "This promises to be interesting. Are we going to get clinical here?" He looked at her hopefully.

She groaned and leaned her head back. "Not if I can help it."

"You're the one who brought it up."

She looked at him and tried not to laugh. It was no use. He purposely pretended not to understand. "Then I'll be the one to drop it, okay?"

He looked reluctant. "If you must."

"I must." Springing to her feet, she gathered up the magazines. "Let's get to work," she suggested briskly.

He turned in his chair to watch her progress across the room toward the bureau. Her movements were quick and impatient, but they retained a graceful flourish that intrigued him. In fact, just about everything about her tended to intrigue him. Not a good sign.

But what the hell—maybe he was making too big a deal out of this attraction thing. He was moving on any day now. A pretty and intriguing woman wasn't going to stop him. Things like that had certainly never stopped him before. He relaxed just a little bit.

"Now, wait a minute," he said as she pulled open the bureau. "I want to hear more about this. Are you telling me that you're starting to get the baby urge?"

So he did get it, after all. She slipped the magazines into the drawer and turned to face him, feeling slightly defensive. "What do you know about 'the baby urge'?"

He shrugged. "You see it on talk shows all the time. All these women hitting the wall of..." He hesitated, giving her a double take, then went on almost reluctantly. "The wall of thirty-five and suddenly deciding they want babies the way other people decide they..." He licked his lips, then decided to go all the way. "The way they want a cute puppy they see in the pet-shop window. The way men go for sports cars, women seem to go for babies. I have never understood it."

He looked at her, expecting anger, but she was laughing.

"No. Obviously you don't understand it at all," she said. "Otherwise you wouldn't make such a ridiculous comparison."

Ridiculous comparison or not, the whole thing made him uneasy. She couldn't be serious about wanting a baby—could she? Thirty-five seemed to be a real hurdle for a woman to get across. It was too bad. But today was her birthday. That was probably it. She was just reacting to some natural melancholy. The thing to do was to help her through the day. Tomorrow she would probably forget all about this aberration.

She stood leaning against the bureau, looking at something on the far wall, her full, warm lips curved in a vague smile. He couldn't tell what she was thinking about. She looked much less formal in her stocking feet and with her hair hanging in casual disarray. Her square-cut clothing didn't reveal much of what was beneath, and for a moment he found himself speculating. She was appealing in a strange way that tugged at his senses.

"Tell you what." He got to his feet and faced her. "Let's go out and get something to eat. What do you say?"

She looked at him in surprise. "Oh, I couldn't...."

"You could." He took hold of her hand and smiled down at her. "Come on, birthday girl. No more working tonight. Let's go out and celebrate."

She risked a look into his eyes and immediately regretted it. "I have work to do," she objected, but her voice wavered and his grin grew more confident.

"Loring's isn't going to fall apart if you're not there shoring up the dike for one night," he told her. "Go put on a party dress. After all, how often are you going to turn thirty-five? You'll never have another chance to celebrate it."

He was right. She felt naughty. She felt sinful. She was finally ready to throw aside hard work and see what having fun might be like. Suddenly her heart felt lighter. "All right," she said softly, her eyes luminous with anticipation. "Wait here."

She felt in a whirl and he stood right where he was, still seeing how her eyes had looked in those last few seconds. Why wasn't he breathing? This was absurd. He put his hand over his heart and gave it a sharp pat, as though he were jump-starting it.

"A one-way ticket to Tahiti," he muttered, turning to wander about the room and survey the knickknacks. "That'll cure what ails me." And he frowned fiercely, just to remind himself how strong he was when it came to avoiding emotional entanglements.

A page had fallen out of one of Lisa's magazines. He bent to pick it up and stared into the laughing face of nine-month-old. "Grow up, kid," he muttered, staring down at it. Lord, she really thought she wanted one of these noisy, messy, drooling things. Pictures were all very well. This little tyke, for instance, looked cute as the dickens in this picture. But just let him in your lap... Memories assailed him—memories of unwashed babies with full diapers and runny noses, whining for something from him that he couldn't give. He blinked quickly, pushing the recollection away. A woman like Lisa was too bright and ambitious to want to get sidetracked by children. If he had to find a way to point that out to her, he would.

Lisa stared into the mirror as though she were seeing through a doorway into the past. It was her mother's closet she had ransacked for this dress rather than her own. She hadn't even bothered to look through her own things. She had party dresses that she hadn't unpacked yet, but without even thinking about it, she knew none of them would do for tonight. Tonight was suddenly special. Something in the air, something in the feel of the night, made her long to dress up, made her want to be...like her mother.

That thought shivered through her like an inspiration. When she was growing up, the main point had been to be as little like her mother as possible. It had been common knowledge around the house that her mother was a vamp who had seduced her father away from his responsibilities and taken him off to the Caribbean where they had both been killed in a boating accident. Her mother had lived for fun and excitement and the next party. But Lisa was never going to be like that. Lisa was smart and hardworking and was going to be a credit to her family. At least that had been the agenda according to Grandfather. Things hadn't gone entirely according to plan, but the goals and values drilled into her head by her grandfather were still very strong in her. She'd never wanted to be like her mother—until tonight.

Her mother's closet was full of clothes that were twenty-five to thirty years old. Why her grandfather hadn't gotten rid of them all years ago she couldn't imagine. But she was glad. And here she was in a tiny black cocktail dress with straps as thin as reeds and a skirt as snug as a stocking.

She laughed softly, looking at herself. She would never fill the dress out the way her mother had. She was thinner than her mother had been, less buxom. But all in all it didn't look ridiculous. In fact, it looked pretty darn good.

Twisting her hair up she pushed in a few pins and took the curling iron to her wisps at the sides, until ringlets framed her face. She found earrings in her mother's box— long, dangling cylinders of gold that caught the light. They were perfect.

She was excited now. She hadn't done anything like this in years. Suddenly she remembered Carson's near kiss in the basement that afternoon. She pressed her fingers against her lips and wondered if he would try to kiss her again.

"Yes," she told herself softly, staring into her own eyes. And then she was laughing. It felt so good to laugh. It made her feel younger.

Her heart beat quickly as she came down the stairs. The dress that had seemed so right in the mirror suddenly felt hopelessly wrong. She was taking a chance, dressing like this. It wasn't really her. What if he thought she looked like a clown?

Carson was waiting at the bottom of the stairs, but his face was hidden in shadow and she couldn't read the expression in his eyes. She stopped midway down the steps and smiled uncertainly.

"What do you think?" she asked, then immediately regretted it. Nothing like broadcasting the fact that she had lost every shred of self-confidence.

He didn't reply. Why wasn't he saying anything? Her heart sank. He saw right through this, didn't he? What did she think she was trying to do, anyway? Be the vamp her mother had been? Absurd. There was no hope there.

She turned, ready to run back upstairs and strip off the horrible dress, but before she could take the first step, he came out of the shadows and found his voice.

"I think . . ." His smoky gaze took in every inch of her creamy bare shoulders, every bit of cinched-in waistline, every provocative curve. "I think thirty-five is really something to celebrate."

He couldn't have said anything more calculated to coax the smile back onto her face. Her confidence returned in a rush and she gave him a saucy smile and posed before coming on down the stairs. She laughed and made a quick pirouette in front of him before opening the hall closet for her coat. One last glance at the store's books sitting on the table, and she shrugged away the feeling of guilt. She was going to go out and have fun, just for one night.

Turning with her coat in her hands, she smiled at Carson. "Isn't this something? It was my mother's. I've never worn a dress like it before."

He took the coat from her. His eyes were burning with a new light that made her tingle. "It's certainly a change for your image," he said softly.

She laughed again, warmed by his obvious appreciation. "Just for tonight. Tomorrow, it will be back to the sensible shoes and the grindstone."

She caught her reflection in the hall mirror just before Carson slipped the coat over her shoulders and hid the dress from view. The dress, the hair, the look ... For just a moment, a wave of sensation assailed her, leaving her breathless—the sticky sweet smell of gardenias in the air and the creamy feel of lipstick on her cheek when her mother bent to kiss her before going out on the town. Time stood still as she remembered the past so vividly, it might almost have been happening again.

"I'll get the car," Carson said, but she hardly heard him. She was still staring into the mirror, living in the past, seeing her beautiful, carefree heartbreaker of a mother with her husky laugh and the flirtatious way she slipped her blond pageboy back and looked over her shoulder. What would it be like to be a woman like that? The kind of woman who made men's heads turn; the kind of woman who could change the course of a man's life.

Six

Lisa tried to shake away those thoughts with a toss of her head and went out to join Carson. But the drive into town was mostly silent.

Carson watched her out of the corner of his eyes. She had surprised him with the dress, the hair, the sexy walk. Surprise—hell! She'd stunned him so badly he was practically tongue-tied. Was this really the same person who had pressed those huge glasses back on her nose and insisted she wanted to save Loring's no matter what it took? It was a bit unsettling to know there was another woman entirely living inside that gorgeous body. He was beginning to feel outnumbered.

"Where are we going?" she asked.

"The Yellow Crocodile, unless you want to go down to Santa Barbara."

"No, the Yellow Crocodile will be just fine. I've never been there."

The place was smoky, loud and dark, with occasional bursts of brilliant light that flashed out when least expected. The doorman looked them up and down.

"We're pretty much packed," he shouted above the noise, his bored face exhibiting genuine disinterest in their fate. "I don't know. You can go on in if you want to share a table with someone else. Otherwise, forget it until after ten."

Carson looked at Lisa and she laughed. Of course, they would share a table. It had been so long since she'd done anything like this, there was no way she was going to turn around and go home now.

"Okay," Carson shouted back to the doorman. "We'll share."

The doorman left his post reluctantly, but he led them inside and pointed out a table near the stage where the band was producing most of the noise. They threaded their way between gyrating bodies. Here and there a face lifted in greeting. Half the place seemed to know Carson.

Suddenly a hand reached out and snagged Lisa's wrist.

"Hey, you. Remember me?"

She looked down at the man who had stopped her and despite everything, she smiled in recognition. "Mike Kramer," she breathed, staring at the face that hadn't changed in twenty years, despite the thinning of the hair on top and the widening of the girth below.

He blinked at her, frowning. "My God," he said at last and struggled to his feet. "Jeez, Lisa, I never realized before how much you look like your mother."

She smiled at him. "Neither did I." Then she remembered just who Mike was and how she felt about him at the moment, and the smile evaporated. "Well, we're supposed to be going out to share that table by the stage."

"No, no, no!" Mike was bubbling with delight at seeing them. His eyes sparkled and he fairly bounced up and down on his toes. "You gotta stay with us. I insist. We'd love to have you. Wouldn't we, Joanne?"

Lisa turned to look at his female companion. She was pretty—a young redhead with a vivacious smile. "Well, sure, Mike," she replied in a kittenish voice that was just this side of cloying. "Your friends are always welcome."

But she wasn't looking at Lisa. Her gaze was riveted on Carson, and Lisa quickly realized he was staring back at her.

"Hello, Joanne," Carson said, his face totally devoid of expression. "How are you?"

Joanne sighed before answering. "Better, now." And then the vivacious smile was back. "Much, much better." She reached out and took Mike's hand in hers.

Mike had been busy commandeering a waiter and he had missed their little exchange. Lisa looked at him quickly and knew he had no idea Joanne and Carson knew each other. Her instincts told her he was not going to be pleased. This didn't feel good. She looked around, hoping to spot two empty chairs at some other table.

"Well, well," Mike said heartily. As he turned his attention back to the others, they all took their seats. "Here we are." He grinned at Lisa, then laughed loudly enough to drown out the music. "No, wait!" he cried, jabbing a finger in the air at her. "I get it. This is your subtle and delicate way of letting me know you're ready to sell out, isn't it?"

Lisa glared at him indignantly. She had known this wasn't going to work. "What?" she demanded. His obnoxious grin was infuriating.

"You came here tonight to let me know that I won. Right? I get that old mausoleum after all."

Lisa drew herself up, her eyes steely cold, and thought of her grandfather. "No way, Mike Kramer," she told him enunciating each syllable.

"What do you mean, no way? You know you can't handle that place on your own." His eyes widened and he turned to look at Carson. "But you're not on your own anymore, are you?" he murmured almost to himself, his eyes glittering and crafty. "You've got James on your side."

Carson met his gaze and held it. "Lisa is in charge of Loring's. I'm just watching out for the bank's money. She's perfectly capable of running things herself." His own expression hardened. "And she'll do that just fine as long as she doesn't run into sabotage from her competitors."

Mike examined Carson for a moment, and then he laughed. "Hey, it's a jungle out there. You gotta be tough." His grin flashed Lisa's way. "Anyway, Lisa and I are old pals. We understand each other. We were sweethearts way back when."

Lisa sat back and forced herself to remain calm. Mike was and always would be an infuriating man. Why did she let herself rise to his bait? She liked the way Carson had responded. She had to learn to stay cool the way he did.

"Didn't she tell you?" Mike was saying. "We were toddlers together."

"Yes," she conceded with just a touch of acid in her tone. "You used to stomp on my sandcastles."

Mike shrugged and looked at Carson as though appealing for justice. "The woman never could take constructive criticism."

Before anyone had a chance to reply, Mike threw an arm around the redhead's shoulders and drew her tightly up against him, as though he were establishing territory. "This, my darling Lisa, is the woman who is going to bear my children. Isn't she beautiful?"

Lisa smiled politely at Joanne. Did that mean they were going to get married? It would seem so. But then why were Joanne's eyes still glued on Carson? Obviously, they had known each other rather well sometime in the past. Lisa felt the stirrings of unease and chided herself. She was just out to have a good time tonight. Carson didn't belong to her. It would be ridiculous to begin imagining things.

Mike was babbling on about how wonderful Joanne was, but no one seemed to be listening until some sort of message flashed from Joanne's eyes to Carson. The woman turned to Mike and cooed, her ruby-red lips forming a seductive pout, "But what happened to my Pink Lady? I never did get a refill."

Mike was up and away, hunting down the waiter, and Joanne turned back.

"Well, Carson," she said, staring at him so hard, Lisa felt as though perhaps she'd become invisible.

"Well, Joanne," he returned, his eyes flat and expressionless.

"So."

"So."

"I haven't seen you out on the town much lately."

Carson nodded. "That's probably true. After all, I haven't been out on the town much lately."

She blinked as though she didn't quite get it. "Ah. That must be why, then."

His mouth twisted. "Bingo," he replied, gazing at her with a look that said he had no intention of tripping down memory lane with her at this moment.

Lisa shifted uncomfortably, wishing she had the right to grab Carson's hand the way Joanne had grabbed Mike's. So far, the woman had hardly acknowledged her existence, and there was something stirring deep inside her that wanted to let Joanne know in no uncertain terms that Carson did have a date.

Lisa looked up at Carson, and a hard, painful knot developed in her stomach. It was more obvious than ever that he and Joanne had once known each other pretty well. How well? For how long? And what were the feelings that lingered?

It was none of her business, but she wanted to know.

Suddenly Carson shifted his gaze from Joanne to Lisa and he smiled. The smile was warm, intimate, enveloping. Lisa sat back and felt the knot dissolving inside her. That was all she had needed.

Joanne saw the smile and her lovely green eyes narrowed. Mike returned with her drink and sat down beside her, but she didn't seem to notice.

"I'm surprised you're still around," Joanne was saying to Carson. "You were talking about leaving town back when we were dating. And that was months and months ago."

Mike was looking puzzled. He was holding out a drink to Joanne, but she didn't seem to care any longer. He frowned at Carson, then looked at Joanne. "You two know each other?" he asked warily, not particularly pleased with the idea.

Carson's smile was a little stiff. "Yes, we know each other. We're old friends."

"Actually, we were quite an item," Joanne added in a loud stage whisper, as though that would keep it more confidential. "We dated for months."

"Weeks," Carson corrected, looking at her as though he was wondering how he could possibly have lasted that long in the relationship. "It was more like weeks."

Joanne's eyes flashed. "Well, it seemed like months to me," she parried. "But now..." She enveloped Lisa in her warm, sunny smile. "Now I have found myself a wonderful man." She patted Mike's short, stocky arm. "A man who is grown-up enough that he isn't afraid of commitment," she said a bit more loudly. "A mature man who wants children... a family. A tender, loving man who understands what a woman needs."

She ended on a note of triumph, and Carson's neck was beginning to turn red. Lisa had a sudden intuition that his much-admired calm was about to crack under pressure.

"Let's dance," she said quickly, tugging on his hand. "Come on. It's a slow one."

He looked up at her blankly, as if he didn't remember quite who she was. When she tugged harder, he rose and seemed ready to follow her, though he did turn back to glare at Joanne one more time.

She managed to maneuver him away from the table before he could say anything more to the woman. The dance floor was crowded, but she felt natural in his arms as they swayed to the music. His eyes had a glazed expression and his jaw looked tight. She smiled. At least he didn't seem to harbor any lingering affection for the woman. But, just to be sure, she decided on a little chitchat.

"Joanne is really beautiful," she ventured. His arm stiffened around her.

"Yes, she's very beautiful," he replied shortly.

Lisa nodded. Silly, but she would have loved it if he had disagreed with her. "Such long legs," she commented.

"Yes," he said again. "Long, long legs."

She gritted her teeth. She couldn't go on cataloging all Joanne's charms. But apparently he wasn't going to volunteer anything on his own. She was going to have to come right out and ask him.

She hesitated. This was a bit nosy. "Be brazen," she told herself silently. After all, he could always just say no.

"Why . . . why did the two of you break up?" She leaned her head back so that she could into his face and try to get an idea of how her question was going over.

"Hmm?" He hesitated. For a moment she thought he wasn't going to answer her. "Well, let's see," he replied at last. "I think it was because she was looking for a husband. And that was something I had no plans of being."

That wasn't the answer she had been hoping for. They danced in silence for a moment, and she wondered if he had said those words as a warning to her. If so, she ought to...do what? Reassure him? Take it as a joke? Or go back and cry in her beer? Making a quick choice, she smiled up at him teasingly.

"So it's just as I thought. You make it a policy to stay away from women who are looking for mates. Is that it?"

He was calming down. His arm loosened around her again and he almost smiled. "That's right."

"Well, what about me?" she probed.

He blinked, looking down. "What about you?"

"I'm looking for a husband. Or maybe you hadn't noticed."

He grimaced. "I noticed, all right. But we're not exactly going out, are we?"

It was her turn to blink. "What do you call this?"

His eyes were hooded. "A business meeting."

She stared up at him, openmouthed, and then a gleam of humor revealed itself in his eyes, and they were both laughing. Despite everything, she felt strangely close to him at that moment. His arm tightened around her and she let her head relax against his chest, her face so close to him, she could hear his heartbeat. He was taking smaller steps, and she could feel his warm breath in her hair. Temptation overpowered wariness and she closed her eyes and let herself settle against his hard, warm body.

Only for a minute, she promised herself. But time stood still.

She was floating. What were those reasons, again, for keeping her distance from this man? She couldn't quite remember. They didn't matter right now. Not tonight. Tonight she was celebrating her birthday, and her mother, and life in general.

This morning she had asked for a man. You never did get exactly what you wanted, did you? She'd wanted a man for all time, someone to head a household. Instead, she'd been given Carson James. But at the moment, she had to admit, she was anything but sorry.

She let herself float, let herself sink into the spreading sensation of his warmth, his hand on her back, his heartbeat beneath her cheek—

Suddenly she realized that the music had changed. The couples around them were bouncing around like kids on hot sand. Lisa pulled back and looked about groggily. She wanted to ask what had happened. She felt as though she'd been under some sort of spell.

"Carson?" She gazed at him, but he looked strange, too.

"What is it, Lisa?"

His hand was in her hair and he was looking down into her face with a look of wonder in his eyes. Her heart began to thump in her chest. My God, she thought crazily. There's something very special about this man.

His gaze held hers for much too long. Neither of them spoke, but there was something communicating between them, some wordless sense of connection that left Lisa's heart beating very quickly, and that made Carson swear softly under his breath before he could force himself to look away.

He was melting, and that wasn't good. He could feel the meltdown proceeding despite all his efforts to stop it. This

woman, with her softness and quirky smile, was getting to
him in a way he couldn't allow. There was more going on
here than simple physical attraction. If he didn't watch out,
he would find himself falling for a woman whose expecta-
tions were just too high for him. He ought to take her home
and get out of her life. He ought to insist on working with
Gregory Rice from now on.

No, that wasn't good. He would have to make those res-
ervations for Tahiti as soon as he got home. A nonrefund-
able ticket. That was what he needed. And from the way
that glacial lump in his chest was melting, he'd better get it
quick.

"We—we'd better go back," he said.

He was drawing back, pulling away. She nodded, letting
his hand go and turning so that he wouldn't be able to see
the disappointment in her eyes. For just a moment, she had
thought...

"Yes, let's go," she managed to throw out cheerfully.
"Back to our favorite couple."

As they threaded their way through the dancers, she held
that moment of closeness to her, savoring it. She knew
Carson wasn't the man she needed in her life. But what if
she could change him? What if she could be like her mother
and turn him around? What would it take to change a man
like him? The knack for it should be in her genes somewhere.

She giggled, squeezing Carson's hand, and he glanced
back at her before pushing on through the crowd—back to
Joanne.

Lisa hated that he and the lively redhead had once had a
relationship. However, there seemed to be hardly a trace of
affection left between the two of them. All she'd seen signs
of was Carson's indifference and Joanne's need for a sliver
of revenge. Which meant Carson had broken off the af-

fair, just as he had implied. The thought made her feel just a bit better—though she knew she had no right to feel anything. She was just being silly. She didn't want a man like Carson. She wanted a man who was ready to settle down. She wanted a man like . . . Mike.

"Argh," she said.

"What was that?" Carson asked, looking back.

She grinned at him, shaking her head. "Life isn't fair, is it?" she remarked.

He took her seriously. "Life is what you make of it," he told her almost sternly, folding her hand into the crook of his arm and looking at her with eyes so blue, they could have been part of the sky. "You've got to make the right choices."

What would you say, Lisa responded silently, only expressing what she felt with her eyes, if I chose you?

But he didn't notice. He was turning to smile to someone in the crowd who had called his name. Lisa sighed. She couldn't choose Carson. He wasn't on her menu. And she wasn't on his.

"Star-crossed lovers," she mumbled idiotically as she continued to follow him through the crowd. "Victims of tormented destinies. Casualties of fate."

"What are you muttering about?" he asked, pulling her close and looking down at her. "I can't hear what you're saying."

She liked being close to him. She'd never noticed before how nice it felt to have a man hover around her protectively. After all her years of holding her own professionally in the marketplace, she would have thought herself beyond such regressive feelings. But she wasn't. She had to fight back the urge to snuggle into his shoulder and bat her eyelashes.

"Here we are," she said instead, looking down at Mike and Joanne. They'd arrived back at the table and there was no more time for private conversation.

Carson held her chair, then took his own, and they both glanced warily across the table to where Mike and Joanne were acting like lovebirds. They waited, but the billing and cooing didn't seem to be headed for a natural ebb. The constant baby talk was bad enough, but when the two of them began to sing old love songs in unison, Lisa and Carson looked at each other then toward the exit.

Joanne turned and smiled brightly at them. "Oh, you two, we just can't help it. We're so excited about getting married and all, we just get silly."

There was no way to dispute that. Lisa nodded and tried to think of something else to ask about. Since this seemed to be her day to be nosy, she might as well go for broke. "Mike mentioned children. Are you planning to jump into parenthood right away?"

"Absolutely." Joanne turned in her seat to give Lisa her full attention. "I'm planning on having four, at least. Two boys and two girls." She giggled. Her need to confront Carson seemed to have faded. "Two little Mikes and two little redheaded females. Won't that look cute?"

Lisa smiled noncommittally. Horror stories had been based on thinner fare.

But Joanne was just warming up. Having babies seemed to be a favorite topic of hers. "I want to have as many kids as I can right now, in my most fertile years. Don't you think that's the thing to do?"

Ouch. That one stung a bit. Lisa tried to smile. "Some of us aren't lucky enough to have the chance to have children that soon. A lot of women are waiting until their thirties, or even, in some cases, their forties, to have children."

Joanne nodded vigorously. "Yes, but don't you think that older women are shortchanging their children?" she countered, and Lisa sat forward, ready to argue that point, but she never got the chance.

Before either of them could say another word, Mike had jumped in. "Don't talk baby stuff with Lisa," he told his bride-to-be. "She's a businesswoman. What does she care about babies?" He grinned wickedly. "The little lady wants something from me, and I'm going to give her what she wants tonight."

They all watched, startled as deer facing headlights, as he paused dramatically. Lisa was almost afraid to find out what on earth he might be talking about. Leaning forward, he attempted to look earnest. At any other time, Lisa might have laughed at the hypocritical picture he made.

"Lisa, darlin', I'm going to give you some advice. The fact is, I'm truly worried about you. You and Loring's, that is."

Lisa stiffened. "Don't be," she said shortly.

"No, really. I care about you. So I'm going to help you. I'm going to tell you the secret of my success."

"Mike..."

He raised a hand to stop her protest. "Here's what you got to do to make that store work for you. You've gotta go with what's today, what's now—glitter and dazzle. They don't care about quality and substance any longer. They want thrills. Cheap excitement wins out every time. Like some guy said, you'll never go broke underestimating retail customers."

Lisa was breathless with the overreaching ego and tastelessness of the man. It was hard to know whether to laugh or cry. "That wasn't exactly how the line went," she choked out.

"Who cares? I know my people. They like schlock. So I shovel it out, and they lap it up. You try to buck the trend, Lisa baby, and you'll get trampled by the stampede toward Kramer's latest extravaganza. Believe me, you can't win."

"We'll see. Give me a chance, Mike. I'll talk to you again in six months."

He shook his head as if he were really upset about what the future held in store for her. Motioning for her to lean closer still, he continued in a loud stage whisper, "I'm going to tell you a little secret, just because I feel sorry for you. This coming Monday we've got a big day planned. We are—" he glanced around to see if any eavesdroppers were hanging about. "—replacing all our male mannequins with real men. Models. Good-looking ones. We sent down to L.A. for 'em. The women of this town are going to go nuts."

She almost groaned aloud. The man was a jerk, but he was also a genius. How on earth was she going to compete with that? He had a corner on all that was bright and captivating and mesmerizing. What was she going to do? Copy him and come in a pale second? That wouldn't do it. She needed something all her own.

Ideas that had been rolling around in her head bobbed up once again. Mike was going for the flashy side of human nature. What could she go for that might counter it? When people stopped being entertained by the new and exotic, what did they turn to?

An idea was beginning to crystallize in her brain. Funny, it seemed to have been simmering there for days, but she hadn't had a moment free to look at it. She frowned, trying to bring it fully into focus.

"Get 'em in the door," Mike was raving on. "That's what it's all about. Once you get 'em in the door, they won't get out again without leaving some of that green stuff behind."

He was right in his way. But his way wasn't hers. She couldn't go for the flamboyant, flashy gimmicks he went for. She had to stay true to herself and what she believed in.

Wetting her dry lips with her tongue, she allowed the ghost of a smile and spoke very softly: "You know, Mike, you just might have something there."

He leaned closer, his dark eyebrows drawn together, as though he were trying to read her lips. "What are you saying?" he demanded.

She smiled. Yes. The more she thought about it, the better it seemed. "Nothing, Mike. You just kind of helped an idea get in my head."

"You say you've got Jell-O in your head?" He roared with laughter. "Oh, honey, I don't think you're stupid. I just think you can't run a department store in the black, that's all."

Lisa looked at Carson. He was sitting on the edge of his chair, his jaw tight again. His eyes said, "I'll hit him if you want me to," but she laughed and reached out to cover his hand with her own.

"Not necessary," she told him aloud, as though he had actually spoken the offer. "Didn't you hear what Mike said before? He and I understand each other." She turned her smile on the whole table. "In fact, he's given me just the help I need in deciding what to do to save Loring's. Thank you, Mike. I won't forget this."

He blinked at her suspiciously, his face strangely drawn and pale now that all bravado was wiped away. "What did I say?" he demanded. "You're not going to try to beat me to the punch with the male-models idea, are you?"

"No, Mike. Male models are not quite my style." Her smile was friendly but secretive. She turned back to Carson. "They're playing another slow one," she murmured, leaning toward him with a twinkle in her eye. "Want to risk it?"

He was smiling at her. He had no idea what she was talking about with her goading of Mike, but he liked it just the same. "I'd risk just about anything with you," he replied, lying through his teeth and rising to help her up. "Let's go."

The ocean breeze tasted like seaweed. It nipped at her bare shoulders until she pulled the coat tightly around her, and it tore at her hair, trying to destroy her upsweep along with her temper. The ocean looked inky in what little moonlight there was. The white foam on the waves appeared oddly fluorescent and menacing.

"When I was a little girl, I had the run of this beach," she told Carson as they walked on the cold sand. "I knew every sea gull, every sand crab."

"A regular California girl," he said.

She turned to look at him. They'd taken off their shoes and begun this trek through the moonlight ten or fifteen minutes before, and he hadn't made a move to touch her. Maybe she wasn't going to get that kiss, after all.

"You're not from around here, are you Carson?" she asked him curiously.

He gave her a brief smile before turning back into the wind. "No. I've only been here for a little over a year."

She considered his answer for a moment. "Where is your home...your family?"

"I don't really have any family to speak of." He coughed and didn't look at her. "Not anymore."

She wanted to reach for him, make him turn and face her. "What do you mean?"

"I mean..." He sounded almost annoyed, as though she had been badgering him. He shoved his hands deep into the pockets of his slacks. "I mean I've got some family, but I'm not much for get-togethers. We're kind of...estranged."

She sighed. She'd sensed that there was something of the sort in his background. "That can be a big mistake. Family is very important. I've always wished I had more family."

He frowned, moving impatiently. "You had family. You had your grandfather."

"Yes. And I voluntarily turned my back on him, the only family I had. It horrifies me now, to think that I did that."

He turned finally and looked down into her eyes. "So you want to make up for it by having a baby?" he asked her softly. "Is that how it is?"

She tilted her face so that the breeze was brushing her ringlets back and she could look up at him unobstructed. Her feelings for her grandfather had a little something to do with this need she felt growing inside her. But that wasn't the whole story, by any means. How could she possibly explain it to him? He seemed so opposed to the very concept of babies. Was it really the baby thing that bothered him so? Or was it the concept of family? Or fear of commitment?

It was a cinch he wasn't going to volunteer the answers. She was going to have to dig.

"I'd love to have a baby," she admitted, a sparkle of mischief in her eyes. "But I was thinking of getting married first."

He wanted to groan, but he stifled the impulse. "How conventional of you," he said dryly.

"Yes." She nodded thoughtfully. "I find that I'm much more conventional than I ever thought I was."

He looked out at the waves and hunched his shoulders. Tahiti was out there somewhere—too far away to see, but not too far away to head for.

It was late. He should get out of here. He'd done his good deed for the night, taking Lisa out on the town for her birthday. He glanced back at her out of the corner of his eye and mentally kicked himself. Good deed, hell. He'd had a wonderful time with this woman. She'd been soft and tempting in his arms, fun to talk to, interesting to watch. Right now he knew that if he turned and looked at her, he would kiss her, and then . . . then . . .

Okay, he wanted her. So what? He'd wanted a lot of women in his time. It didn't mean a thing. And in the old days, he probably would have gone ahead and kissed her and asked himself in for a nightcap and things would have proceeded from there.

But this was different. She'd been very honest about what she wanted. And he hoped he had been just as honest in letting her know there was no way he was going to get involved in a serious relationship. So it was best to keep his hands off. That way nobody got hurt.

He glanced at her. She was standing with her chin high and her eyes closed, reveling in the salty ocean breeze. Her eyebrows were arched perfectly above her lovely eyes, their dark lashes sweeping over the high cheekbones. Her lips were slightly open. She looked pure and untouched, waiting for something or someone to make her complete. For the first time in his life he felt the tug of that same need, that yearning to be half of a whole. Startled, he jerked his gaze away and took in a deep breath of cool air.

"Tell me more about your family," she said before he had a chance to say something biting that would serve to distance them from each other.

He stopped, surprised again. "There's nothing to tell." He half turned toward her, glowering. "You're really hung-up on this family thing," he grumbled.

"We all come from families," she retorted. "They're pretty basic."

He shook his head, his eyes dark. "Not to me, they're not."

She hesitated, searching his eyes, but he wasn't about to reveal any clues there. Without saying anything, they both turned and started walking back to the house.

"What exactly do you have against families?" she asked at last.

"I had enough family when I was growing up," he answered gruffly.

She let herself drift close enough to bump against him companionably as they walked, and then she wondered why he wouldn't even put an arm around her shoulders. "I thought you were an only child."

"I was. But my father was...gone a lot. I ended up living with relatives. Lots of relatives." He turned to give her a quick look. "And I'll tell you something about family. No one knows how to stick the knife in and twist it like a blood relative."

So that was it. He had family. He just didn't like them much.

"I don't know," she mused as her house came into view, its Victorian exterior looking slightly spooky in the shadows. What a great house that was going to be for Halloween parties. She could picture ghosts hanging from the eaves, a huge jack-o'-lantern on the porch, the front door creaking. And children laughing with delicious fright. "It might be different if you tried making one of your own."

He rubbed the back of his neck with his hand. Yeah. It would probably be worse. "Not on your life," he said almost cheerfully. "Not for me."

She sighed as they came up on the sidewalk. So much for her career as a molder of men. "Then I guess you're really serious. You won't be in the market for fathering a baby anytime soon."

She said the words so wistfully, he felt a slight rush of adrenaline. She was scaring him, for God's sake.

"Me?" He sounded startled, a little horrified. "No. Not at all."

She shrugged and made a face, as though sincerely sad to hear it. "I didn't think so. I guess I'll have to scratch you off my list."

He looked at her sharply. She was teasing and he knew it. He couldn't resist the hint of a smile he saw in her dark eyes.

"Oh, I was on it, was I?" he asked, not quite as grudgingly as he had spoken before.

She nodded, flirting a bit with her eyes. "In the 'tentative' column. Just below one world leader and two famous rock stars."

His eyebrows rose. "Below? What have they got that puts them ahead of me on the list?"

She grinned at him. "Nothing, really. I just knew them first."

"Right." He laughed. She was doing it again, making him feel warm and toasty inside. She seemed to have a knack for that. "And just who is on your nontentative A list at this point?"

"No one." Her brows knit in a slight frown and she caught his gaze with her own. "That list is absolutely blank."

He stared back at her for a moment. "Good," he replied, his voice slightly muffled. "That ought to tell you something, don't you think?"

Slowly, she shook her head. "I'm not going to give up," she said so softly he could hardly hear her above the sound of the waves. "And I don't have time to mess around."

And that was just the point, wasn't it? The longer he stayed, the more danger there was that they would "mess around." He'd thought they could see each other without too much risk just as long as they both knew the score. He'd been wrong. Dancing with her, holding her in his arms, had taught him quite a lesson.

There really was no free lunch. If he didn't want to get chewed up himself, he was going to have to stay away. That was all there was to it. He stirred uneasily. "I guess I'd better be going," he said, turning abruptly.

"Wait. Carson?" She stopped him with a hand on his arm and he turned, swallowing hard before he could look at her. "I wanted to tell you something. I have an answer for the question you asked me this afternoon."

He nodded, waiting.

"You wanted to know why I wanted to save Loring's. Okay. Here goes." She took a deep breath. "Loring's was created by and nurtured by my family. If I let it fail, I give up on my family. If I make it succeed, I give new life to everyone—Grandfather, my mother, my father, all of them. And I create a legacy for my own children."

He was impressed. There was no doubt that this came from the heart.

And then her face took on an impish look and she added, "And one more thing. I'm bound and determined to kick Mike's you-know-what."

He laughed, wanting to reach for her. But he couldn't. With the parameters they had set up, she was out-of-bounds.

Her face was shining and he had no doubt she was fully committed and emotionally involved. He'd already seen it in her eyes when she'd challenged Mike. She was in this fight to the finish. That meant he would have to stay around, at least until she got things rolling. Moving involuntarily, as though controlled by some force he couldn't stop, he raised his hand to brush her hair out of her eyes, and the next thing he knew he was leaning toward her, his hand curling around her chin. He was going to kiss her. And if he kissed her, he was going to stay longer....

"I've got to go," he said gruffly, and yanked his hand away, forcing himself to step backward.

She stood very still, her eyes huge in the moonlight. "Thank you for everything," she murmured as she watched him leave. "I had a wonderful time."

He hesitated at the corner of her house. "So did I," he called back. And then he was gone.

Her shoulders sagged. He didn't want to kiss her. That really took the edge off the evening. Maybe the sense of connection she'd been feeling was all in her head.

She turned slowly and moved toward her front steps. There on the porch was the doll buggy with the Baby Aboard sign. A passerby must have pushed it in close for safekeeping, thinking it belonged to someone in the house.

She stopped to look at it, running her hand over the handle. There was something so sad about the empty bed, the unused pillow. No baby aboard. There was a lot of that going around these days.

But she wasn't going to mope. Whipping out her key, she unlocked her door with a firm click and pushed it open. Her birthday was over. It was time to go in.

Sighing, she began to step inside.

"Lisa."

She looked up with a start, just in time to see Carson coming toward her, taking the front steps two at a time.

"Lisa, I forgot to wish you one last happy birthday," he said.

His eyes were dark as the midnight sky, full of mystery, but she didn't care. As his arms came around her, taking her up as though she were something he couldn't resist, she lifted her face to his in a gesture that was anything but surrender.

His kiss was hard, almost angry, and it caught her up like a wave hurtling toward a storm-tossed beach, taking her breath away, scaring her, thrilling her. She clung to him, holding on to his heat, his excitement, the dark, rich taste of his mouth, and marveling at the deep, insistent yearning that was beginning to grow inside her.

He wanted her. She could feel his desire, and she responded as she never had before, from somewhere deep within. This had nothing to do with finding a father for her baby or searching out a qualified man. All that mattered was the clean, male scent of him, the pounding of his heart, the hot, liquid feel of his body against hers. She was riding a wave of pure sensation, holding on for dear life.

Just what Carson had been afraid of was happening. Things were about to spin out of control. Her response surprised him. After all, they had only met that day. In many ways, they barely knew each other. And yet she welcomed him as he deepened the kiss, moving closer, pressing her hands to his chest. His body came alive with a lack of control he hadn't felt since he was a teenager, startling him. He drew back first, staring down at her, and she smiled up at him, her eyes misty, her lips looking slightly swollen and very provocative.

He didn't know what to say. His throat was closing up, his mouth was suddenly dry. The kiss had been a revelation. He was already attracted to her; had been from the first. But that kiss had been a little too much, too soon, and he almost felt like apologizing.

Lisa looked at him questioningly, not sure what was bothering him. But he hadn't said a word and she didn't want to be the first to speak.

His large hands still held her shoulders as he drew her back close to him, and bending down, he whispered near her ear, "Happy Birthday, Lisa." His lips gently brushed her cheek, and then he backed away. In a moment he had disappeared into the shadows again, and this time he really was gone.

Lisa stood very still, holding the heat for as long as she could. All in all, it had been one of her very best birthdays ever.

Seven

Carson sat staring at the airline ticket on the wrought-iron poolside table before him. It was a warm day and the pool area was crowded, but he hardly noticed the laughter and the shouts of the others.

"One way to Tahiti," he observed, fingering the colorful protective folder. There it was in black-and-white—and assorted other colors. The reservation was confirmed. The fee was paid in full. He was ready to go.

It had been almost two weeks since he had decided it was imperative that he take off for the islands as soon as possible. For two weeks he'd been working side by side with Lisa Loring, and for two weeks it had been just as she'd promised: all business. The sweet, provocative lady he'd escorted to the Yellow Crocodile—the woman who had scared him so much he'd almost forgone a birthday kiss for fear of finding himself locked into something he couldn't control—had disappeared and left behind the Lisa of the huge round glasses and the rapid-fire directives and the sudden suspicious frowns. The funny thing was, it didn't make any difference. He felt a clear and present need to get himself to Tahiti as quickly as possible.

There was something about the woman he couldn't resist. It was hard to believe that after all these years, he would find himself fascinated by a woman who criticized his ideas and glared at him through glasses that made her look like a country schoolmarm. And a woman who wanted to get married and have a baby. That was even worse. How could this have happened?

He'd known men who got married—sad, lost souls who wandered around the supermarket buying baby food and adding up their charges on pocket calculators, hoping to fit food into a budget swallowed up by the monthly mortgage payment. They wore milk stains on their silk suits and pretended they couldn't tell that the hideous wailing sound that filled the place was coming from the infant ensconced in their own shopping cart.

He'd seen these people and he'd gone on his way, laughing up his sleeve, happy to know that he would never, ever, find himself in such a ridiculous predicament. He'd never understood why other men subjected themselves to that kind of torture. The love of a good woman was worth a lot, but not that much.

But now, for the first time in his life, he was beginning to get a hint, just an inkling, of why a man might give up his freedom and commit social suicide by marrying and having a family. Just an inkling. By no means did he fully understand it. And if he could only get out of here and get to Tahiti, he hoped he'd never have to.

There was just one little detail that bothered him. He'd had affairs over the years—casual flings, torrid weeks of passion, mature sexual relationships. He'd been kissed and tempted and made love to and seduced. Often, the experience had been wonderful. But as he looked back, the incidents tended to blur, one into another. Not much stood out in the long run. So why was it that his one gesture of physical affection for Lisa, that one quick, fiery birthday kiss, stayed with him like a brand on his soul?

Disgruntled, he looked around him at the crowd of residents and their guests sitting around the swimming pool. Sally walked by and waved. Carson waved back, but didn't give her a look that might have encouraged her to linger. Sighing, she shrugged and moved on to a group of laughing young men who were more receptive. Carson watched and scolded himself severely. He knew he was acting like an idiot. Sally was exactly the sort of woman he needed in his life. Fleetingly. And that was just the way it should be. So what was wrong with him? Why couldn't he summon up the slightest interest in the girl?

Stretching back in the reclining chair, he let the sun bake his tanned body. He had to get conditioned for Tahiti. That sun down there was relentless. He would swim, go fishing off the reef, take an outrigger into the open waters.

And then Lisa crept into his thoughts as she always seemed to lately. Lisa and her soft, dark eyes. What would Lisa be like in Tahiti? Would she lose that frown and deep-six those glasses? Lisa in a grass skirt—no, even better, Lisa in a sarong, her silver hair cascading down her back, strands of it braided with orchids, her arms and feet bare. He closed his eyes and let himself enjoy her that way. The picture made him ache. They knew how to live life in the islands. If he could just get her to Tahiti—

"Hey, mister."

He knew that voice. He opened one eye. Sure enough, Michi Ann Nakashima stood beside the table, her ornery yellow cat in her arms. He closed his eye again. Maybe she would think he was asleep. Breathing very slowly, he waited and hoped.

But Michi wasn't going for it. "Hey, mister," she repeated, just a little louder.

He opened both eyes this time and stared straight at her. "The name is Carson, Michi Ann. Carson James."

"Hey, Mister Carson James," she said, adjusting effortlessly. "Can you help me with my cat?"

Carson looked at the big old cat stretched like a limp doll in the little girl's arms. The golden eyes stared back at him with unblinking malice. Carson winced. What had he ever done to this animal?

"What's the matter with old Jake?" he asked reluctantly.

"He's got a hurt foot," she told him. "Could you look at it for me?"

Carson stirred uneasily in his chair. The scratches on the backs of his hands were almost fully healed. There were other adults sitting around the pool, dozens of them. Why was she always coming to him?

"I don't know, Michi Ann. Your cat hates me."

Those big brown eyes were as clear as ever.

"No, mister. You're the only one he likes."

"Likes?" He glanced at the malevolent face, then looked again, harder. Was the animal grinning? He almost shuddered. Frowning, he moved edgily.

"What about your mom, Michi? Women are so much better at these nurturing things."

"He likes you, mister."

"Does he?" His gaze met her open, trusting eyes and he caved in once again. "Oh, all right," he said gruffly.

The cat's eyes seemed to crinkle at the edges and then the corners of its mouth seemed to stretch into a wicked grin. Carson frowned and swallowed hard. He was going nuts.

It was only an animal. He wasn't going to wimp out here. His lips thinned.

"Bring him closer," he instructed, reaching for Jake. "I'll take a look."

Lisa chewed on the end of her pen and watched Carson out of the corner of her eye. Greg was droning on and on about fiscal figures and five-year austerity plans, going back over things they had covered a hundred times, and she'd lost interest long ago. Martin Schultz, the head buyer, was asleep. Terry was doing a crossword puzzle. And Carson was doodling on the cover of his address book. She'd already heard the proposals Greg and Carson had worked out together—plans to cut staff to the bone, plans to jazz up advertising, plans to reduce product lines—all sound in the face of disaster, none very exciting or optimistic. And she'd already decided what few parts of them she would take under consideration and what major parts she would scrap out of hand.

She just hadn't quite figured out how she was going to tell them. Her own ideas were still forming in her mind, but she was pretty sure she was going to go with a totally new approach. They weren't going to like it. But this was her department store, wasn't it?

Sink or swim, that was about the size of it. Either her idea was going to work, or there was going to be no more Loring's. In any case, she needed a quick fix, a blitzkrieg of a change, something that would come in and sweep away the cobwebs and make Loring's the place to be once again. And then...and then she would be free to concentrate on her private goal.

She glanced at Carson again. He was looking especially handsome today, in a navy blue sport coat with dove-gray slacks. He had a nasty scratch along the side of his nose that made her wonder if he'd been in some kind of accident—or maybe a fight. She hadn't asked him about it. She was trying not to care about his personal life.

He looked up and caught her studying him. She frowned and looked away. She'd been frowning at him a lot lately. He deserved it. When you came right down to it, he was ruining everything.

Not the plans for renovating Loring's. Though they argued about details, he was actually quite a help with the big picture.

No. Where he was the most trouble, where he spent his entire time muddying the waters, was in her love life—that nonexistent flame she was trying to kindle from the ashes of neglect. The fact of the matter was, she had recently discovered that there was quite a stock of eligible men in this town. As she had begun to make the rounds of the chamber-of-commerce mixers and backyard business barbecues, she had been meeting men, nice men; men who had been divorced and missed being married; men who had lost wives and yearned for the old companionship; men who had reached an age and a maturity where they had finally decided it was time to settle down. She should have been in heaven. Opportunity was knocking on all sides.

But lurking in the background there was always Carson. He was turning up more often than a guilty conscience.

The evening before had been a case in point. She'd stopped by a wine tasting she'd been invited to by the mayor, and before long she'd found herself monopolized by Andy Douglas, a local dentist whose wife had left him to try to make it on the Broadway stage. He was sort of cute, with a friendly smile and a loud, hearty laugh. He leaned close and kept trying to refill her glass, while she kept emptying the contents into the flowers. He caught her at it. They laughed a lot, and he began to tease her gently, knowingly. Any other night it might have led to larger things. But just when she was having the most fun with Andy, she saw Carson, who had just arrived, leaning against a far wall, watching her.

He never came over. He never said a word. But for the rest of the night, she couldn't get the image of his dark, brooding face and those piercing blue eyes out of her mind. She went right on laughing, but her heart wasn't in it any longer. And poor Andy. He probably never did understand why she'd turned him down when he'd asked her to go with him to dinner the next evening. And come to think of it, neither did she.

Carson was always talking about how he could hardly wait to leave for Tahiti. Here's a bit of news for you, my dear, she thought, glaring at him from across the conference table. I can hardly wait until you leave, either.

For the first day or so after their night out together she had clung to the ridiculous hope that he might change, that something about her might change him. She'd had an absurd dream that she might follow in her mother's footsteps and mold a man into what she wanted.

Carson had doused those hopes in no time, making it perfectly clear that he wasn't moldable. He hadn't changed a bit. He didn't want to change. Why should he? He was perfectly happy the way he was—a restless heart. So be it.

"Excuse me, Miss Loring," Carson said suddenly, startling her out of her reverie. "I hate to disturb your train of thought, but I would like to get a look at those charts you're guarding there, by your elbow."

"But of course, Mr. James," she answered with the same exaggerated courtesy. Picking up the stack of papers, she pushed them down the table toward where Carson was sitting. "If you happen to think of anything else I can do that would make your life more comfortable, please don't hesitate to let me know."

His blue eyes were hooded. She wanted to look away, but she wouldn't let herself. This was the way it had been for days now. They communicated politely for a while, and then one of them would say something that seemed to set the other off, and the searing remarks would fly. It was almost as though they were in the middle of a long, sustained battle, but neither one of them was really sure what they were fighting about. It was true. They were incompatible.

And it was such a crime. She'd never met a man she could respond to the way she could to him. When she thought about the kiss, she shivered inside with a special ecstasy she'd never experienced before. She knew she would never find that with any other man—not so long as Carson himself was around to remind her of what she was missing.

If only he were a different sort of man. If only there was even a chance that he might see the light and embrace the prospect of family life. But she knew his prickly behavior was meant to guard against just such an eventuality. And that was why she treated him likewise.

But if only—if only—her eyes half closed as she worked with what she had, translating him into a fantasy dad, putting him into tweeds and giving him a warm, tender manner. There he was, sitting by the Christmas tree. The lights were twinkling. A fire was roaring in the fireplace. A huge fluffy dog lay at his feet, looking up at him adoringly. Laughter was heard in the hall, and then in tumbled the children, three of them, all dressed in white flannel nightclothes. Daddy Carson smiled and held out his arms to them. Shrieking with happiness, they raced for their father's embrace—

"Lisa? Lisa?" Greg was shaking her shoulder. "Are you all right?"

She looked up at him groggily, reluctant to let go of the lovely picture she had conjured up in her mind. Greg was staring at her strangely. So was just about everyone else around the table.

"I guess I've just hit overload," she admitted with a small smile. "Let's call it a day, shall we? We can go on from here tomorrow."

There was a murmur of general agreement and the others began to pick up their papers and prepare to depart. Lisa left first, her arms full of ledgers, but before she had gone more than four steps down the hall, she found Carson was by her side.

"You're working too hard," he said accusingly. "You should take some time off. You need a rest."

"Who, me?" She glanced at him and shifted the books to her hip. "Don't worry about me. I get plenty of rest."

"Oh, yeah?" They stopped to wait for the elevator. Carson swung around so that she had to face him. "Those six hours of sleep at night don't count," he said. "You need to get out and do something to take your mind off this business." He hesitated, then charged ahead. "How about tonight? Why don't you join me for a little dinner at the Shell Steakhouse?"

She stared at him. This was the first time he had even hinted at a possibility of going out with her again. Her heart was in her throat and she was tempted. Dinner with him—talk, laughter, maybe even another kiss. A tremor flashed through her.

She took a deep breath. "Sorry," she told him crisply. "I'm busy."

Something shifted in the depths of his gaze—something wild, something that made her feel chilly. His jaw tightened. "You're going out with Andy Douglas, aren't you?" he asked softly.

She knew how she ought to answer his question, but she was beyond that now. "It's none of your business," she said quickly. "But no. I'm not."

He looked skeptical. "I heard him ask you last night."

She stuck her pen in the knot of hair she'd pulled together at the back of her neck and looked at him coolly. "Well, I guess you missed the part where I turned him down."

He still didn't look as though he believed her. "Don't you like him?"

That was rather direct. "I...I like him very much." Her chin was lifted defiantly, challenging him to do something about it—anything at all.

He took a deep breath. His piercing blue gaze still held hers. "Then why aren't you going out with him?"

She knew she should tell him to mind his own business. She knew she should tell him to stay away from her and not to eavesdrop. But she didn't tell him anything. Instead, she stood very still, staring into blue eyes that stared back. There was no point pretending, even to save her own pride. It was all very well to act defiant, but what did she have to protect? If he could read her mind through what he saw in her eyes, he would know why she couldn't go out with Andy. The question was, would he care?

The elevator arrived. She forced herself to turn away and enter it. Carson stayed where he was, and she didn't wait. He could take another elevator. He could take the stairs. It was all the same to her.

The next morning they were back around the conference table again and Lisa was feeling a bit restless herself. They were wrapping things up as far as preliminary studies were concerned. The surveys had been made. The results had been tabulated. Charts and graphs had been drawn up and explored. It was time to come up with a final plan and go for it.

Lisa looked down the table at Carson. How much longer would he be sitting in one these meetings? What would she do when he didn't come around anymore? She saw him reach inside his suit coat and finger his airline ticket. He carried the thing around with him as though he thought it would protect him from harm or something. A talisman. Maybe she needed one of those herself.

"What on earth is all that racket?"

Until Greg made his complaint, she hadn't even noticed the raised voices outside the conference-room door. Glad of a break, she rose quickly.

"I'll check it out," she said, walking to the door and throwing it open. Outside in the lobby she found Garrison, baby Becky poised on her hip as usual, talking excitedly to the secretaries and clerks who gathered around her.

"Garrison, what's going on?" she called.

Garrison came rushing toward her, her face alive with excitement. "Oh, Miss Loring, you wouldn't believe it! I've just been over to Kramer's. They've got those male models back, and guess what! They've got female models, too, this time. And I swear they're all half naked. The women are in bikinis or lingerie or worse. They walk around and smile at you and want to show you the clothes they're wearing and tell you what department you can get them in, but the kicker is, most of them don't have on much more than a G-string. So what are they trying to sell you? Your guess is as good as mine."

"It sounds..." Words failed her.

"I know. Isn't it just about the tackiest thing you've ever heard of?" Garrison crackled with delight. "I'm going back over. Want to come take a look?"

Lisa was still slightly overwhelmed. "I— Not right now, thank you." She steadied herself. "But Garrison, when are you coming back to work?"

Garrison shifted the baby and sighed. "I'm dying to come back, Miss Loring, but everyone else in my family is gone all day and I just can't bear to leave Becky with strangers. If I can just find someone I can trust to watch her..." She waved as she headed for the elevator.

Lisa turned back into the conference room. It was immediately evident that they had all heard Garrison's news. There was a buzz going around the table, and she was sure she heard the word *bikini* at least twice. Before she had a chance to say a thing, Carson cleared his throat, evading her eyes, and said, "I'm afraid I'm going to have to... go out for a little while. I have something I need to do."

Lisa gasped at his transparent disloyalty. She slammed her hand down on his briefcase before he could get it up off the table. "You're going over to Kramer's, aren't you?" she accused, glaring at him.

He glared right back. "So what if I am?"

"I can't believe you could be so immature. You're going over to see half-naked models, aren't you?"

A spark of simple triumph lit in his eyes. "Does that bother you?" he asked softly.

It bothered her, all right. But she would die before admitting it. "Of course not. I just hadn't realized you were still so adolescent."

He nodded slowly, his eyes gleaming. "I can be very adolescent when the mood strikes. It's one of my salient characteristics."

"I have no doubt about that." She glanced around the table, realizing they had a very attentive audience. "Well, go if you must." She waved a hand airily. She would have loved to add, "half of the models are probably old girlfriends of yours, anyway," and would have if the others hadn't been listening. Instead, she flashed Carson a sizzling look that said it all. "Say 'Hi' to Mike for me."

He started toward the door, then thought better of it and turned back. Looking down into her rebellious eyes, he hesitated, then shook his head and said reluctantly, "Look, it may reassure you to know there is more to this than ogling bimbos. Someone has to keep abreast of the competition's moves, don't you think?"

She narrowed her eyes. He had a point there. She hadn't been inside Kramer's since she was a little girl. How could she fight something she didn't even know? "You're absolutely right," she answered slowly, eyes sparkling. A smile was growing between them. "I'm going with you."

"Really?" He couldn't hide his satisfaction.

She nodded, studying him speculatively. "Yes. Really."

Neither of them paid the least attention to anyone else in the room. It was as though they had forgotten the others were there. Carson reached out and took her hand in his. "Let's go," he told her. And they were out the door.

At first Lisa declared she would go to Kramer's proudly and openly, not trying to hide her identity like the spy she'd thought Carson was when she first saw him. But a bit of reflection changed her mind. She would feel like such an idiot if Mike saw her.

"Disguises are easy," Carson reminded her. "You've got a whole store full of things to choose from."

In the end she picked a black bobbed wig, dark sunglasses and a fake fur. Carson chose shades as well, and wore a baseball cap and a black leather jacket. As they walked through Fine Jewelry they couldn't resist matching gold wedding bands. "We're Candy and Chet Barker from Las Vegas," he told her, making her laugh. "We're here visiting a maiden aunt."

He slipped the ring on her finger and she giggled. She felt like a kid playing hooky. They went across the street and joined the throng crowding to get into Kramer's. Just the sight of all the people was depressing after the empty aisles at Loring's.

Once inside the store, they stood in jaw-dropping awe. The place was a revelation. Colors, light and sound jumped out at them from all sides. Television monitors showing rock videos were set everywhere. Banners flew in each department, with large, colorful symbols of what was on sale. A voice on a loudspeaker broke in every now and then, cracking a joke and announcing quick, limited bargains. The models were as shocking as Garrison had described them, wearing gauzy bits of cloth that hardly covered a thing, stopping to dance in sexy gyrations when a good beat sounded from the video screen. The customers loved it. Kramer's was Now. Kramer's was Happening.

"And we're just yesterday's news," Lisa said softly, clinging to Carson's arm. "We have so far to go."

He nodded. He couldn't tell Lisa now, but he didn't hold out much hope. Mike Kramer was a promotional genius. How was she going to fight this? He tried to think of something comforting to say to her, but before he could form a decent idea, a voice from behind stopped him in his tracks.

"Hey, mister. Remember me?"

He turned and looked down at his little cat-owning friend from the condo. She was looking up at him with her usual earnest appeal. So much for the disguise. He frowned in disgust.

"Michi Ann. How did you know it was me?"

She looked slightly puzzled, as though she couldn't imagine why he would ask such a silly question. "I saw you and I came over to say hello," she explained quite sensibly. "Look at my new shoes." She stood with her feet displayed in their shiny new Mary Janes.

"Yeah, those are great." Carson wasn't sure of the exact etiquette involved in praising new shoes. Avoiding the issue, he turned to include Lisa. "Michi Ann Nakashima, this is Lisa Loring."

"How do you do?" Michi Ann greeted politely. "Do you have a cat?"

"A cat?" Lisa smiled at the darling little girl. "No, I'm afraid not."

"You could get one if you want. They have cute new kittens downstairs in the pet department." Michi Ann looked at Carson, her eyes wide and unblinking. "You should get one."

Carson's smile was forced. "I'm afraid I can't keep a cat, Michi Ann. I'm always moving from place to place."

She nodded. "Us, too, since Daddy's been gone." Her eyes clouded. "But see, that's what's good about Jake. When we go to a new place and I get sad because it's kind of scary and I don't know anybody, it's okay, because I always have Jake. He's my very best friend." She favored Carson with one of her rare smiles. "You could do that, too, if you had a cat like Jake."

Carson's first reaction was to find and throttle anyone who would make this child sad. Memories of childhood misery brought back the feelings of how it had been for him. Without thinking through what he was doing, he dropped to his knee so that he was face-to-face with her, pulling off the dark glasses so that she could see the sincerity in his eyes.

"I'm your friend, too, Michi Ann," he told her quietly. "Don't forget that. Okay? Whenever I'm in town, I'll be there for you, just like Jake."

"Sure, mister. I know." She nodded solemnly, then lifted her head. "My mom is calling me. Bye, mister." And she was off in a flash of petticoats and new shoes.

Carson rose slowly, feeling just a little numb. Lisa turned with a questioning glance into the depths of his dark glasses. "I thought you didn't like children," she stated as they continued their stroll through the store.

"I never said I didn't like children," he responded defensively, his hand pressed lightly to her back to guide her through the crowd. "I merely said I preferred life without them."

"I see." She smiled. She liked the hand against her back. She liked his closeness, his square jaw, his confidence. For no known reason, her heart was light despite the depressing evidence of Kramer's success.

"Hey, all you shoppers," the loudspeaker announced suddenly, Mike's voice booming above the sound of rock music. "We have a special treat today. Lisa Loring of Loring's Department Store is here, shopping in our store. How's that for a compliment, huh, folks? Even Lisa Loring knows that our store is the best. Thanks, Lisa. But the black wig isn't you, honey. Why don't you visit our beauty salon? Our girls will fix you up with something spectacular. Hey, it's on me, Lisa!"

Carson held her hand very tightly as they made their way quickly toward the exit. Lisa was muttering swearwords she'd never spoken before. Carson was laughing.

"This isn't funny," she cried, pulling the collar of her coat up around her ear and praying that no one else would recognize her. "I hate that man! I have to beat him, Carson. I just have to!"

He sobered. From what he'd seen today, and over the past two weeks, he didn't think that was going to be possible.

They went back across the street and took off the fake fur and the wig and the leather jacket. Lisa held her hand up to the light, looking at how the gold band shone against her finger. Glancing up, she saw Carson watching her. He had pulled off the band he wore and put it back into the case. He was waiting for her to pull off hers. A perverse impulse made her close her fist and turn toward the elevator instead, with the ring still on her finger. The moment she had made the move, she felt ridiculous. But she wasn't going to back down now. For just a while, she was going to carry that ring on her finger and let herself dream.

Back in the jewelry department, Carson hesitated, looking down at the ring. It looked really good against the black velvet. Suddenly, illogically, he reached for it again.

Chelly was working the counter and he turned to her. "I'm going to keep this out a little longer. Okay?"

She shrugged and gave him a sly look from beneath her long sable lashes. "I've got your receipt, so I'll know who to come to for money if it doesn't come back," she replied archly.

He dropped it into his pocket and turned away, then almost walked into a wall. Which only fit the crazy way he was acting. What the hell was he doing? He was carrying around a wedding band, for Pete's sake. Why? Why?

Because Lisa had kept hers. But that didn't make any sense. He wasn't going to get married. He wasn't even going to pretend to be married. So, what the hell did he need a wedding band for? If he could, he would have taken it back, but he had a feeling Chelly would be on the phone to half the store in no time if he did.

So, what else was new? That was probably where she was right now, anyway. He stood indecisively in front of an open elevator, unable to come up with a plan of action. He might have stayed there for hours if Greg hadn't come up behind him.

"Come on, let's go. Lisa's called another meeting in the conference room," he said briskly.

Carson nodded and followed him onto the elevator, the wedding ring burning a hole in his pocket.

Lisa was waiting in the conference room. She gave them all a quick rundown on what was going on at Kramer's. "They're creaming us," she stated flatly. "And from the looks of things, we can never hope to compete on the bright, jazzy level they've taken over as their own. All we would do would be to come in a pale second if we tried it. Therefore..." She paused and took a drink of water. "Therefore I've decided we are going to go in a completely different direction. Kramer's is aiming to be synonymous with flash. We will aim for family. In the long run, I'm betting family values are the more enduring ones."

There was murmuring in the ranks. She knew they weren't going to embrace her idea wholeheartedly at first. But she pushed ahead, outlining her basic plan. "We'll change our name to Loring's Family Center. Every department will be revamped to put family needs at the top of its priorities. We'll start a day-care center for our employees, and eventually I hope to have one for the shoppers, as well. Our baby section will hire a full-time nurse who will set up classes in child care. Juniors will hire a counselor who will also put out a newsletter with an advice column. Our goal will be to make ourselves the one-stop shopping place for all modern family needs. And, by the way, instead of laying off half our employees, we'll cut prices to the bare minimum and go for volume to pick up the slack."

She went on for another hour, getting very little feed-back but laying out her thoughts and ideas so that they could mull them over, then give her their reactions. Her first impression was that no one was too crazy about her plan. That made her shaky, but she was going to stick to it. She really didn't see any other choice.

"I guess that about covers it," she said at last. "I've got that Rotary dinner tonight at Le Château, so I'm going to have to get going. Think things over and we'll discuss this again in the morning."

The one face she most wanted to read when she was fin-ished was Carson's, but his eyes were expressionless. He might as well have kept on the dark glasses for all she could see in them. His opinion was the one she valued the most. What did he think?

He rose and gathered his things, and for a moment, she was afraid he was going to leave without saying anything. But he came past where she was standing, leaned close to her ear, and murmured, "You're bound and determined to carry this family fixation you have to a high art, aren't you?"

She looked into his face, ready to argue, but a reluctant smile lit his eyes. "You just might pull this off, Lisa Lor-ing," he told her. "Too bad I won't be here to see how it goes over."

Without another word, he turned and left the room. Lisa stood frozen. Relief mixed with regret. It wasn't time for him to leave yet, was it? Not now. Not when everything was still so up in the air. A dull ache began to throb in her chest. What was she going to do without him?

Carson stared into the bottom of his glass and told him-self he was going to regret this evening. He had a wildness in him tonight, a need to take chances.

He was standing in the courtyard of Le Château, the finest French restaurant in the area, where the Rotary was about to have their annual dinner. All the movers and shakers in town were there. Gerald Horner, the town's leading industrialist, was busy lecturing him on coastal development. But his mind was on Lisa, who was standing at the far end of the yard next to the fountain, and was surrounded by men. He couldn't stop looking at her. She was having much too good a time.

Why did he keep coming to these things? He'd started going at first because he had thought he could help her out. She was new in town; he could introduce her to people, get the social ball rolling for her. Of course, his presence had been totally superfluous from the first. The men were drawn to her like moths to a flame. She didn't need him at all. So why was he here? To sit through another mediocre meal, listening to people he didn't want to be with babble on about things he didn't care about?

He glanced at Lisa. Her head was thrown back and she was laughing. It was time to form couples and go on into the dining room. Obviously she was juggling offers right now, making the big decision as to whom she would partner at the table. He ran a hand through his hair and moved restlessly, trying to keep from looking at her. What did he care? Let her sit by anyone she chose. It didn't matter to him.

He emptied his glass and grimaced. Who was he trying to kid? If he didn't care, what the hell was he doing here? He cared, all right. He wanted to be with her. So why didn't he do something about it?

As he watched, she reached up to push her hair back behind her ear and the gold wedding band flashed in the lamplight.

"Eureka!" he whispered, smiling to himself. He dropped his hand into his pocket and there it was: the matching ring. Slipping it on his finger, he nodded to a rather startled Gerald and excused himself, turning to push his way toward the crowd around Lisa.

As he reached the center of the group, Lisa looked up at him with startled eyes, her silver-blond hair framing her pretty face like a halo. She wore a very feminine dress with a scoop neck that pushed the soft swell of her breasts up high. Something deep inside him responded to her with a yearning very much like physical pain. He had to swallow hard before he could speak, and he stared down at her, ignoring the murmur of voices all around them.

"Excuse me, gentlemen," he said smoothly at last, looking up and smiling at them all with an easy confidence he hardly felt. "I'm afraid I'm going to have to assert a prior claim here."

"Oh yeah?" Andy Douglas protested, moving closer to Lisa as though he were going to grab her and hold on. "On what grounds?"

Taking Lisa's hand, Carson held his up beside it. The matching rings gleamed in the light.

"I hate to disappoint you, boys, but Lisa and I were married this afternoon," he stated flatly. "So I'm sure you can understand that we would like a little time alone."

"What?" Andy Douglas looked as though he were about to suggest pistols at forty paces, but another man held him back.

"What?" Lisa protested, as well. But her reaction was lost as Carson bundled her away and into the dining room.

"What did you do that for?" she sputtered as he led her to a quiet table for two hidden behind greenery, rather than to one of the large tables set for ten out in the center of the floor. She wasn't sure whether to laugh or cry. Did he think this was a good joke, or had he just had too much to drink? "Some of those people might actually believe you."

"I had to do it," he told her, pulling out a chair for her and gesturing with mock gallantry. "It was for your own good."

She hesitated. She should yell at him and turn on her heel and take herself back to the men who were acting so wonderfully attentive. It was a lot of fun to be fought over, and Carson had no right to act like this.

But when you came right down to it, Carson was the only man she really wanted to be with. So she sat down with a pronounced pout, just to let him know she wasn't a complete pushover. As she watched, he came around the table pulling the other chair so that it was next to hers rather than opposite. "How was this little bit of kidnapping for my own good?" she demanded skeptically.

"Well..." He sat down and looked at her, rather content with what he'd done. "It was getting altogether too disgusting watching you dole out your favor like some latter-day Scarlett O'Hara. I couldn't let you do that to yourself."

She stared at him, not sure what she was feeling. "You're jealous," she said softly.

His eyes flashed. "Damn right," he admitted with a rueful look.

She could hardly believe it. It still seemed like a joke. But he looked serious enough. And if he were actually serious—then she should be really angry.

"Now, let me get this straight," she said. "You don't want me, but you don't want anyone else to have me, either."

He looked startled. "Who said I didn't want you?"

She gaped at him. "Why, you did, with every word, every action, in every way you possibly could."

She had him there. He looked down at the silverware, busily moving it over to set a place in front of his new position at the table, avoiding her eyes. "Okay. Maybe I don't want to get serious. But that doesn't mean I want anyone else to have you," he muttered.

"What?" Her reaction was automatic, pure outrage.

He looked up and stated with all candor, knowing how absurd he sounded, but still unable to find an acceptable way to varnish the truth, "As long as I'm here, I don't want to see other men hanging around you."

Rage was emphasizing the pale lines of tension around her mouth. "Then it's a good thing you're leaving soon, isn't it?" she accused.

"Uh..." He looked back down at the silverware. "I wanted to talk to you about that."

"What?" Suddenly her heart was beating very fast. Despite her annoyance at his high-handed manner, she wasn't exactly immune to his charms. If he had changed his mind about leaving...

"I'm thinking of putting off the trip to Tahiti for a few more weeks. I figure with this new plan, you're going to be swamped and I ought to stick around and help you implement it." He looked relieved to have it out in the open. His fingers played restlessly with the fork. "So... what do you think?"

She hated herself for being so happy. Very carefully, she opened her napkin and placed it on her lap. "Oh, I think we could probably handle things without you," she replied very deliberately. She risked glancing up, and something in his eyes made her melt. "But it certainly will be more fun with you around," she added quickly, then bit her tongue.

"Good." His hand came up to where hers lay on the table and covered it as he favored her with a half smile. "I really do want this Loring's thing to succeed, not just because I've been assigned to this case, but because I...I really care about you."

She smiled back. That old temptation was nibbling at her again. If she tried really, really hard, could she change him?

No. Mentally, she slapped herself back down. This one was not for her and she might as well face it. His trip to Tahiti had been postponed, not canceled. Still, she could enjoy what she had of him, couldn't she? The touch of his hand on hers, the sound of his voice, the way one eyebrow rose when he was being especially sincere. Taking a sip of wine, she smiled to herself. Why not?

He was sitting very close and she leaned even closer. "They're all watching from the main table," she informed him. "Don't you think you'd better kiss me?"

She watched for his reaction, holding her breath. What was going on behind the smoky blue of his eyes? He'd said he cared about her. He'd said he was jealous. So why was he still hesitating?

He slid his gaze over her cheek, past the pulse faintly throbbing in her neck to the full curve of her breasts swelling against the lowcut neckline, and he steeled himself. This wasn't going to be easy. Moving slowly, he took the back of her head in the palm of his hand and drew her toward him, avoiding her eyes, keeping his gaze on her full, moist lips. He hesitated just a fraction of an inch away from touching her. He wanted this to be right—polite, affectionate, lighthearted. She couldn't be allowed to feel how much he wanted her.

And then he kissed her. The kiss was brief, friendly, repressed. It answered no questions and left her hungry for more—much more.

She drew away and laughed nervously. He slumped back in his chair and looked away. The silence between them yawned like a black hole.

Lisa was puzzled and disappointed. She'd never known a man who was so protective of his own emotions. Or maybe it was just that she'd misread him badly. Maybe the rest was all talk, and the truth was, he just didn't like her all that much.

She started to talk about something inconsequential, just chattering, and he looked up, listening, and little by little he began to respond to things she said. She was relieved. It was going to be all right.

Dinner was better than usual for such an affair, and they had a good time, laughing and talking despite the lingering tension between them over the kiss. The others seemed to have bought the story of their marriage. They stayed away in droves for the rest of the evening. It would take a while to rebuild those relationships, but she didn't care. The more she was with Carson, the more she knew that it was the only place she really wanted to be.

She invited him to her house for a nightcap, and he compromised by saying he would come for a walk on the beach instead. He followed her home in his own car. The night was chilly, with a fog rolling in. She took off her shoes and pulled her coat tightly around herself and walked beside him in the dark. For some reason, neither of them seemed to have anything more to say, so they walked in silence.

"I heard there's a storm coming," he said at last, stopping to look out into the mist toward where the waves were breaking against the shore.

She came up beside him. "I can feel it," she murmured. "Can't you?"

He looked down at her and made a slight movement of impatience. "You feel too much," he chided gently. "Cut it out."

She stared back at him, the wind off the ocean slapping her hair across her face. She thought she knew what he was asking. He wanted her to back off, to help him maintain this pretense that they meant nothing to each other.

"I *want* to feel," she told him. "That's what life is all about. Emotions are for real, and I want to experience them all. I want to really laugh. I want to really cry." She lifted her chin defiantly, her eyes dark with anger. "And when I get kissed, I want to know it."

He turned from her, picked up a round stone and threw it hard, far out into the waves. "Sorry if my kiss wasn't good enough for you," he replied coldly, staring into the darkness. "I didn't realize you were such a exhibitionist. I thought someone like you wouldn't want to display a lot of embarrassing stuff in public."

"'Embarrassing stuff'?" She grabbed him by the lapels and pulled him closer, forcing him to look back into her eyes. "We're not in public now, Carson."

His eyes had a haunted look. Reaching out, he took her face in his hands. "Don't, Lisa," he said, his voice husky, his face full of denial. "Don't start something we'll both regret."

She slid her hands inside his jacket and flattened them against his chest. His warmth was a tempting contrast to the cold air.

"I'm not afraid," she whispered into the wind, searching his eyes. "Why are you?"

He groaned. The heat from her hands came through his thin shirt like fire against his skin. "Lisa, I swear to God—"

"No," she objected firmly. "Don't swear. Don't think. Just kiss me. Kiss me right."

"Lisa..."

She slid her hands up and sank her fingers into his hair, trying to force him closer. Throwing his head back, he closed his eyes, and she pressed her lips to the pulse point at the base of his neck. She felt his groan rather than heard it. It rumbled through him, and then his arms came around her and his mouth found hers, and she was spinning into the waves again.

Carson kissed her hungrily, afraid of what was coming, determined to keep control, but not sure how hard he was going to have to fight for it. Her mouth tasted better than anything he'd ever known, sweet and silky, warm and rich. The scent of her skin was musky and he reached out to gather more of her to him, sliding his hands beneath her coat, wanting to explore whatever he could touch. He slipped his hands down and took hold of her, pressing her against his hips.

Was that her voice he heard—that small animal cry of pleasure? He used his mouth to answer, his tongue exploring the sweet depths of her, his lips caressing hers with tender insistence. He wanted her, every bit of her. He wanted her touch, her body, her need. He felt as though he had waited so long—much too long—as though he would die if he didn't have her, right here, right now.

But this was insanity. He had to stop. Pulling away, he took in a deep, ragged breath and tried to calm himself. His eyes were dark with turmoil, his face pale and hard in the foggy night. He held her face between his hands and shook his head, looking at her, devouring her features with his untamed gaze.

"God, Lisa," he managed to rasp out. "If I was going to let myself get involved with anyone, it would be you."

And then he dropped his hands and turned to leave.

Lisa was in shock. How could he be leaving? How could he reject her this way? She knew he wanted her as much as she wanted him.

Still gasping for breath, still trying to make sense out of what had just happened, she watched him disappear into the fog. Was what he had just said supposed to make her happy? Was it supposed to satisfy her? Rage began to bubble up in her throat.

Turning, she stumbled back to her house, steadying herself against the handle of the little carriage that still sat outside, waiting for its owner to return. The Baby Aboard sign slapped against her hand and she touched it with her forefinger. If she left things up to Carson, this was as close as she would ever get to having her dreams come true. It wasn't good enough.

Eight

Carson turned down a corner of the page on the paperback he was reading and tossed it into the chair across the room as though it were a basketball headed for a three-pointer.

"And the crowd goes crazy," he muttered to himself as he rose and started toward his kitchen for a drink of water. "They're chanting his name. 'Carson, Carson, Carson.'" Filling a paper cup at the faucet, he drank from it, crumpled it in his hand, spun and aimed at the wastebasket for an encore. "Carson does it again. The man is incredible."

He looked around for something else to throw, but the only things left on his counter were the toaster and a dozen eggs he had left out when he'd cooked himself an omelet for dinner. He considered the carton of eggs for a moment, but decided against it. What if he missed? He'd have a real mess to clean up.

A blast of wind from the storm shook the building and the lights flickered. Dropping back down onto the couch, he switched on the radio and turned to an all-news station, coming into the middle of a report on the weather.

"... battering our coast tonight. High winds combined with unusually high tides have prompted the Department of Public Safety to call for an evacuation of the homes along the oceanfront. Flooding has been reported..."

Swearing softly, he turned from the radio and picked up the telephone, dialing Lisa's number for the fifth time since he'd come home from Loring's. Busy. How could it still be busy? And why the hell didn't she have Call Waiting?

He wouldn't put it past her to have taken the phone off the hook just to torture him. They'd been sniping at each other all day. He knew she was angry about what he'd said the night before, how he'd run from her. Didn't she understand he was doing it for her? Did she really think he enjoyed denying himself what he wanted more than anything in the world right now?

The first thing he had done that morning was to take the wedding band back to the jewelry department. Lisa's band was already there, gleaming in the black velvet tray.

"What is this I heard this morning about you and Carson being married?" Greg was asking her as Carson came into her office.

She looked up and saw him. "That's right," she said brightly to Greg. "We were married for a little while last night." She sighed, ignoring his strangled gasp. "But it didn't last. The honeymoon was sort of rushed. We never did learn how to connect with each other the way you're supposed to. Then, later in the evening, we got a quickie divorce." She waved her hand with its bare ring finger. "So now, everybody's happy." She turned and gazed coolly into Carson's eyes. "Carson is just like one of those lions in that movie about Africa. He's gotta be free. Like the wayward wind, he was born to wander. Isn't that right, Carson?" she challenged, acid dripping from her tongue.

He sank into a chair and grinned at them both, unwilling to let Lisa get his goat. "That's about the size of it. She got custody of the Jag, but I did get weekend visiting rights. Now I'm just waiting to see how much alimony she's going to stick me for."

She tried to pretend she hated him, but he could see the gleam of laughter in her eyes. That relaxed him. And though she'd directed cutting comments at him for the rest of the day, and he'd made a few back, he knew, behind all the banter, that she was hurt. Now he only wished he knew what he could do to tell her he was sorry.

Picking up the telephone, he dialed her number again and got the busy signal. Instead of hanging up, he put in a call to the operator.

"All our operators are busy right now. Please stay on the line and our first available operator will be with you shortly. All our operators are busy right now. Please stay on the line..."

It occurred to him then that the phone line wasn't busy. It was probably down. He slammed the receiver back in its cradle and jumped up, grabbing his jacket and heading for the door. There was a major storm attacking their area, and the beaches had been evacuated. He had to make sure Lisa was all right. If he couldn't get her by phone, he would have to go out there himself.

As he drove toward the beach, he began to worry more with every mile. The wind was vicious, coming at him in blasts that rocked his car. Branches were down everywhere. Large pieces of sheet metal were curled around fences and tree trunks. Large chunks of the roofs of the beach houses littered the pavement. This was one monstrous storm.

The car shook, skidding around corners and fighting the wind. The rain hit so hard he could barely see out the windshield at times. Most of the houses along the oceanfront were dark, already evacuated. But there were lights on at Lisa's. Did that mean she was still there?

He left the car in the street and ran through the driving rain toward her back door. Pounding on it, he yelled, "Lisa?" He pounded again. There was no answer. Quickly giving up, he ran around the side of the house and went in through the garden, rattling the French doors until he found one that popped open and let him in. "Lisa?"

Her house was well lit, but he didn't see her anywhere. If she wasn't here, where could she be?

"Lisa?" He went quickly through the living room, the den, the kitchen, the hallway, and then up the stairs. "Lisa?"

The sound of a door opening had him spinning.

"Carson?" Lisa stood in the doorway of her bedroom, dressed in blue silk pajamas that clung to all the right places. Her hair flew about her face like a golden cloud of sparks. Her feet were bare. "What are you doing here?"

He sagged against the wall, partly in relief to have found her, partly in reaction to the way she looked. How much was a man supposed to be able to take? First the emotional tug-of-war with her all day, then the growing fear that she might be hurt or in danger, and finally, this. The shiny blue silk outlined her entire body—her hips so enticingly rounded, the flat, smooth stomach, her full, soft breasts, swaying slightly, the nipples hard and clearly delineated beneath the gossamer cloth. The muscles across his abdomen and down around his hips contracted hard. He felt as though he'd been kicked in the gut.

"I came to get you out of here," he managed to grate out, staring at her dark eyes, frowning fiercely, trying not to let her see what she was doing to him. "Come on. You can't stay here. It's too dangerous."

She shook her head. "Don't be silly. This house has stood for almost a hundred years. One little storm isn't going to destroy it."

He wanted to grab her, throw her over his shoulder and head for the door. Steeling himself, he forced a calm he didn't feel. "There's nothing little about this storm. Trees are coming down all over the place. Your roof could be next." He gestured toward the front of the house. "The tide could be tearing your porch off soon. Everyone else on this block has been evacuated."

She was shaking her head, shrugging away his arguments, and he couldn't stop looking at the way her breasts moved under the shiny fabric. He was going over the edge any minute now. He had to do something. He had to establish control. Jamming his fists into the pockets of his jacket, he said roughly, "Come on. Let's go."

"I want to stay," she persisted, hands on her hips. "This is where I belong."

Was it all in his imagination, or was she purposely challenging him? He'd had about enough of her contrariness for one day. Erasing the distance between them with a few long strides, he pushed open the door to her room and turned her around by the shoulders.

"Get something on," he ordered. "I'm taking you with me."

She recognized the note of command in his voice, and her eyes changed. It wasn't in her nature to be a silly twit, and she didn't want to act like one. If he really thought it was this important, she would do as he said.

"Where are you taking me?" she asked as she pulled open her drawer and took out a sweater and a pair of jeans. She turned to look into his eyes. She'd seen his response to her pajamas. A quiver of excitement shivered through her. If she was going to be spending the night with him . . .

He was watching her gather clothes together, his eyes black and hooded. "To my place, I guess," he answered. "Unless you have someplace else you'd rather go."

"No." She shook her head quickly. "No. Your place will be just fine."

Their gazes met and they both knew what the other was thinking.

"Hurry," he urged softly.

"I will."

But she didn't move. She stood right where she was, looking up at him with her huge dark eyes, asking him . . . A tremor shook him. She was so close, he could feel her heat, smell the scent of her hair. Like a man in a trance, he looked down. Without conscious design, his hand rose and touched her, sliding down the slippery cloth, cupping her breast, his finger curling around the hard nipple; his breath stopped in his throat.

There was no longer the matter of controlling his desire. He *was* desire. All of him, all he was, wanted her, had to have her, couldn't go another moment without her. And he let his hand slide lower, down across her stomach, down between her legs.

She made no move to stop him. There came a sound from deep in her throat, and her hips moved, accepting him while at the same time, she began to unbutton her pajama top. It slipped from her shoulders and fell to the floor with a sound too slight to be heard above the wind.

Carson looked at her pink-tipped breasts and he felt as though there were something large and heavy growing inside his chest. He couldn't breathe. He couldn't think. He could only move toward her, with her, touching her, taking her flesh in his hands. She was soft, softer than anything he had ever held before; but he couldn't stop to marvel at her because the fire inside was driving him. He had to have her. He'd waited too long, and now he had to have her.

They were on the bed and he wasn't sure how they'd got there. His shirt was open and he was shrugging out of his jeans, and when he turned to look at her again, she was completely naked, her skin glowing like gold in the lamplight. He ran his hand across her, touching her elbow, her arm, her breast, flattening his palm against her stomach, sliding it down to find where she waited for him, hot, moist and urgent.

He shouldn't be doing this; he should be stopping himself. Like a drugged man, he looked into her face. Maybe she would do or say something to stop him. But her eyes were wide and deep as limitless caverns, smoky as an autumn landscape, unfathomable as the sea.

"Don't stop," she whispered. "Oh, please, Carson, don't stop."

She was riding the crest of the wave this time, not tumbling in the white water, and she wanted to take it all the way. If he pulled back on her this time, she didn't think she could bear it.

She wouldn't let him go. Reaching up, she dug her fingers into his thick hair and pulled him to her. His mouth came down on hers and she opened to him with a wildness she'd never felt before, as though she could devour him. He moved above her, pressing her back against the spread, and she welcomed his weight, gloried in it.

His body was hard, and as slick and smooth as satin, and her hand trembled as she took hold of him, gasping at his beauty. He groaned and writhed at her touch, trembling with need, and she felt exalted with her power, even though his power over her was just as absolute.

She cried out when he entered her, then again and again as her need built in a frenzied spiral until she thought she would go mad. His breathing was loud and ragged in her ear, and then she was lost in the sensation of joining, and all she wanted was his pleasure and hers to blend and build and go on forever.

It almost seemed to last that long. Even when it was over, she didn't want to let him go. They held on to one another, neither of them saying a word for a long, long time. Tears welled up in Lisa's eyes, and she was glad his face was still buried in her hair and he couldn't see them.

The tears were for the incredible intensity of what they had just experienced. But they were also for the knowledge that she loved him—and that love had to be bittersweet.

Finally he brought his head up and gazed at her. A look of pain crossed his handsome face. "Oh, God, Lisa," he said roughly. "I shouldn't have done that." But his hand cupped her cheek and he dropped a kiss on her lips.

"I wanted you to," she answered simply. "And I'm glad."

He rolled back to look at her and desire flared again, startling him. Lowering his head, he teased her nipple with his tongue and felt the stirring of need begin to ripple through him. She arched back, sighing softly, and was just about to say something seductive, when a loudspeaker blared just outside their window, stopping them cold.

"This block has been evacuated. If there is anyone left in this house, you must leave now. There is no one else left on this block and we cannot guarantee your safety."

Carson's head shot up. "Oh, Lord. I left my car in the street." He stared at her, suddenly remembered why he had come. "Hey, we've got to get out of here."

"No!" She reached for him but he took her hands in his and pulled her up.

"We've got to go. High tide is only an hour or so away. With this wind blowing, there's no telling what might happen."

She rose, still holding his hands. "To your place?" she asked.

He nodded.

She smiled. "All right."

They raced to put their clothes on and head for the back door. There was almost outside when Lisa remembered something.

"Wait." She ran back through the house despite Carson's protest, flinging open the front door and running out into the rain. Where was the little baby buggy that had been sitting in front of her house for weeks now? She wanted to put it inside to protect if from the storm, but as she spun, searching in the night, she couldn't find a sign of it. It seemed to have been blown away.

She ran back and caught up with Carson, ignoring his comments. There was something disturbing about the buggy being gone. She'd felt an odd kinship with it for so long, with its Baby Aboard sign hanging on its empty nest. And now it was gone.

They drove back through the storm. There was almost no traffic.

"Only a fool would be out in this weather," Carson observed with a grin. "Guess what that makes us."

Lisa laughed. She knew she was a fool. She wouldn't be here with Carson if she weren't. But playing the fool felt right for the moment. And that was what she would do.

At one intersection, a large piece of wood came spinning through the air, narrowly missing their windshield. There was no telling where it had come from. Lisa sat back in her seat and began to feel very nervous. Carson was right; this was no little storm.

They had almost reached Carson's apartment, creeping along at a snail's pace in order to see where they were going in the heavy rain. Suddenly Carson stepped hard on the brake, holding out his arm to make sure Lisa didn't hit the dashboard.

"What is it?" she asked.

"Can't you see it? That big old eucalyptus went down. It's blocking the street." Reversing the car, he maneuvered it to the side and parked, shutting off the engine. "We're going to have to run for it."

So they ran. Rain pelted them and the wind tore at their clothing, and whipped the breath from their mouths. But they ran, holding hands, and by the time they reached his apartment they were soaked to the skin and laughing so hard, Lisa was afraid they would never stop.

They clung together, dripping all over his entryway.

"We'll have to strip right here," he said, tugging at her sweater.

"You're right," she agreed, reaching for his belt.

In a moment they were naked again and making love on the carpeted floor, because they couldn't wait until they'd got to the bedroom. She wrapped her legs around him, urging him deeper with her hands and harder with her cries, and he whispered her name as he soared, making her shiver with delight.

His lovemaking was so intense, so pure, so basic, it took Lisa to a level of sensation and release that she'd never reached before. For long moments afterward she felt a sense of fulfillment she had never known. But for some strange reason it didn't seem to last, because almost immediately she felt as though she wanted him again. Was it because she was so unsure whether or not they would ever have a night like this again? Or was it just that he was so good, she couldn't get enough of him?

They got up and took a shower together. Carson wrapped her in his big fluffy blue robe and started a fire. She watched the flames and wondered how it was possible to be so miserable one night, and so happy the next.

Of course this wasn't real I've-found-the-man-of-my-dreams-and-we-plan-to-live-happily-ever-after happiness. This was more a conscious decision to take what she could get. That thought made her frown for the first time since she'd heard him in her hallway.

Carson got up and stirred the fire and she watched him, her throat choking with love and tenderness for him. She liked the way his hair fell over his forehead, the way he looked up, both eyebrows raised, when she said something to him, the way his wide mouth twisted into a crooked smile when he looked at her. She ached for him, for his arm around her shoulders, for his lips on her temple, for his voice, his touch.

She was full of lust for him, but not just for the ecstasy of his lovemaking. She wanted so much more. He sat back down beside her and she sighed as he came close, and burrowed her head in the hollow of his shoulder. This was what she really wanted. His warmth. His affection. His friendship. His *love*.

Had she changed him? She glanced at him out of the corner of her eye and almost laughed aloud. No. He had changed her. He had taken a rather impatient, boring drudge and turned her into a love goddess—at least for tonight. She slipped her hand inside his shirt and ran it across the hard muscles that took her breath away. He groaned, stretching back, inviting more of her touch.

"Here we go again," she whispered in his ear, laughing.

This time he carried her into the bedroom and placed her carefully on the thick bedspread, stroking her hair, her face, her breasts, until she was writhing beneath him, demanding his strength. And still he held back, teasing her, until she cried out, "Love me, Carson. Now!" And then he took her and held her and tried not to notice that the words meant more than the physical act they had just shared.

They lay tangled in the sheets and talked softly in the low light from the hall. Outside the storm raged, battering the walls, the roof, the courtyard. But inside they were warm and close, insulated from the rain and the cold.

"Lisa," he asked suddenly, his fingers playing with her hair, "are you protected?"

She hadn't been the first time, but she'd taken care of things since then. Still, his question chilled her, bringing in the first pinprick of reality since they'd started down this road.

"Don't worry," she said evenly. "I know how you feel about children."

He lay very still, staring at the ceiling. He'd been thinking more of her protection than his own, but she had every right to take it that way. After all, he didn't want children. He wasn't prepared to marry anyone, either.

"Someday," she was saying softly, her hand stroking his arm, "you're going to have to tell me what made you such a grouch where kids are concerned."

He turned and gazed at her. She was so beautiful, she made his heart contract every time he looked at her. Right now, he felt as though he could tell her anything.

"I suppose it's rooted in childhood experiences," she suggested quietly.

"Isn't everything?"

"So the Freudians would have us believe." She rose up on her elbow to look at him. "So, tell me what it was," she went on, tickling him with her soft caresses. "Were you sent off to the circus at an early age? Did the children in the audience throw peanuts at you when you were trying to do your trapeze routine, forever distorting your view of young people?"

He groaned and turned away.

"No?" She smiled, leaning over to keep up the tickling. "Were you raised by wolves? Did you work in a sweatshop in your formative years? Were you lost in the Gobi Desert with a pack train of babies? What?" Bending down, she kissed his naked side and tasted it with her tongue. "What?"

He looked back at her and managed a smile. "Okay," he said, turning away again. "I'll tell you how it was."

Lisa went very still. She had a feeling this wasn't going to be easy for him, and she didn't want to do anything to disturb his memories.

"I mainly grew up at Aunt Flo's. She was my mother's sister, and she had six children of her own. When she found out she was going to have to keep me, she wasn't too happy about it." He winced, remembering. "I can still see her screaming into the telephone, trying to find somebody else to take me."

Lisa fought a growing sense of horror and tried to keep her voice steady. "How old were you?"

"About four, that time." He glanced at her quickly, then away again.

"And you can remember that?"

His laugh was short and harsh. "That kind of rejection sort of sticks with you," he said, then regretted it. He didn't want to whine about his background. Moving restlessly, he tried to think of a way out of telling her any more.

"Go on," she coaxed. "Did you stay with her until you were grown?"

"Most of the time." He answered reluctantly, but looking at her, he knew he was going to have to tell her more to get her off his back. He traced her small ear with his finger and wished he could just make love to her again and forget all this talking.

"Since she was stuck with me, she decided to get some benefit from the deal. The first few years I guess I was just a drain on her, but by the time I was eight or so, she'd figured out ways to use me. I got to take care of the babies. She'd started a needlework business by then—her husband was always out of work and hanging out at the local bar— and she needed someone to watch the kids. She even kept me out of school one year. She told the teacher there was a family emergency. The emergency was she needed babysitting while she ran around setting up her shop."

"How could they let her get away with that?"

He shrugged. "No one questioned it that I know of. So there I was, taking care of the little ones." His eyes had a glazed look. He'd given up trying to resist the memories, and he was seeing the past as he hadn't for a long time. "God, they were dirty, messy kids." Even now it made him feel slightly sick to remember. "Aunt Flo wasn't the best housekeeper in the world to begin with, and there was never enough money to give them good shoes or clothes or even decent food, sometimes." A faint smile played across his lips. "I used to cook hot dogs one night and use the water from heating them to make soup the next night. I'd just throw in scraps from the refrigerator and cook them up with that good old hot-dog water."

"Ugh." Lisa made a face.

"You better believe it. The nastiest stuff you ever tasted. One night I remember all we had was one can of creamed corn for the seven of us. That was dinner." He shook his head. "It wasn't always like that, though. That was mostly the year I stayed home from school to take care of the kids. But a lot of the time, I cooked because I had to eat, too. I must admit I didn't do much cleaning. The place was always a mess, and the kids were filthy. Of course, looking back I realize that was my fault as much as anyone's. They were filthy because I didn't do anything to make things different."

"But you were just a kid."

He nodded. "And not cut out for raising a family," he added. "I hated every minute of it."

This was not something she wanted to hear. She touched his cheek. "What kind of relationship did you have with your cousins?"

He looked at her. "I didn't like them. As far as I was concerned, they were a passel of snotty-nosed brats." His face changed. "All except for Angela," he said softly. "She was different. She was so small and so weak, but she would try to help." A misty smile settled in his eyes as he remembered. "She was like a little mother, you know? Trying hard to nurture plants that refused to grow." He touched Lisa's hair, letting it slip through his fingers. "She was blond, like you. She would sneak me things out to the garage."

"The garage?"

"Yeah. That was where I slept. On nights when Aunt Flo was mad at me and had banished me from the kitchen, if there was something for dessert, Angela would bring me some after everyone else had gone to bed."

He was quiet for a moment, and Lisa steeled herself to ask a question she was almost afraid to hear answered. "What happened to Angela?"

"She died." He said it as though he were announcing the weather, but Lisa wasn't fooled. She recognized the pain beneath his stiff demeanor. "She got hit by a car."

He didn't speak for another long moment. Lisa longed to take him in her arms and comfort the boy who had lost his only friend so suddenly, but she didn't dare. Something in the way his shoulders were set told her to leave him alone.

"And not too much later," he went on at last, "I took off. I was fourteen by then. And without Angela, there didn't seem to be any reason to stay."

Lisa hurt for him; hurt for the little boy who had grown up in such a miserable place. But she wanted to tell him that this wasn't the way it had to be. There were loving families, happy children, clean people who were considerate and caring. That was the kind of family she would strive to have. And surely. . . he would, too.

This wasn't the time to bring up her argument for reassessing the need for children, though. That would have to wait. But a tiny part of her was afraid the right time might never come.

They spent the night locked in each other's arms, sleeping right through the worst of the storm, and in the morning, Lisa didn't regret a thing. At first, Carson didn't seem to, either.

They sat together and drank coffee and giggled and touched. They talked about the storm, and then the conversation drifted back to Loring's and her ideas for the family center.

"You're taking a big chance," he warned her.

"I know." She smiled. "Life is for chances, isn't it?"

He stared at her. He'd never really thought of it that way before. But she'd already gone on to something else.

"Listen, I had some thoughts about restructuring the maternity section. I want to write them down before I forget them. Do you have a piece of paper?"

"Sure." He had risen and started a new pot of coffee. "Go ahead and get some out of the desk." He pointed her to a rolltop on the other side of the living room.

She opened the beautiful old desk. No stack of paper was readily apparent. Rummaging in the compartments, she knocked down three long envelopes, all of them addressed to Carson and bearing a return address in Leavenworth.

Leavenworth. That was odd. Wasn't that where the big federal prison was? She reached to pick them up and the letter fell out of one of them, sliding all the way to the floor. Leaning down, she retrieved it, but her glance couldn't miss the salutation. "Dear Son," it read.

But wait a minute. Carson didn't have a father.

She never read anyone else's mail. She wasn't a snoop. But for once, she let her gaze linger as the paper fell open in her hand. The letter was signed, "Your father, Daniel James."

"Carson," she called softly.

He was running water in the sink and didn't hear her.

Suddenly her heart was beating hard and she was unfolding the paper, reading quickly, skipping from one paragraph to another.

"I can't tell you how much I regret... You are all I have left in this world... You never answer my letters, but I'm not going to give up.... If you would only call me, and we could work to start over again.... I don't expect you to forgive, but if we could just put it behind us... I love you, son."

"Carson," she said more loudly, turning with the paper in her hand. "What is this?"

When he saw what she had, his eyes widened and he came quickly. "Give that to me," he ordered, holding out his hand.

She lifted it up. "No. It's from your father. I thought you said your father was dead."

His eyes were dark, haunted, and he slowly shook his head. "I never said that," he reminded her. "I let you assume it, but I never said it." He winced. "And anyway, he's dead to me."

She stared at him, shaking her head. "Because he's in prison?"

He shrugged. "That's only part of it."

She moved toward him, her hands to his chest, imploring him. "Oh, Carson, don't do this. Did you read this letter? The man is desperate to see you, hear from you. He needs you."

Carson's eyes flashed. "He needs me? Great. Where was he when I needed him?"

How could she get through to him, make him look at his own emotions without the anger, without the bitterness that shielded him from the truth? "Carson, you've got to answer him. You've got to go and see him."

His jaw jutted. "Never."

What could she do to convince him? She looked up into his eyes, trying to convey how important she thought this was. "He's . . . he's begging you."

Carson turned away, unwilling to go on with this, but Lisa followed him, unwilling to let it alone.

"I know about loneliness. I know about bitterness and the need for revenge." It was hard to convince people to put aside emotions. She knew that. Emotions didn't care about logic. They only knew what they felt. "It kept me away from my grandfather for much too long. And how I have regretted it ever since. He's your father. You have to answer him.''

His muscles were tense, the cords in his neck standing out. She knew he hated to have her badger him like this, but she had to do what she could.

''I don't have to do anything,'' he said curtly. ''I don't know who this man is. He keeps writing, he keeps bothering me. But I don't give a damn about him. Put those letters back, Lisa. Or better yet, throw them away.''

She didn't say another word. Turning, she quickly slipped them back into the compartment where they had been and took the blank sheet of paper she had been looking for. Carson was a stubborn man. She was going to have to keep that in mind.

They sat down again and sipped coffee, but it was difficult to recapture the carefree mood they had reveled in earlier. Fantasy had given way to reality. And Carson's regrets had surfaced, too. Speaking carefully, he tried to explain them to her.

''I've tried to fight wanting you from that first night at the Yellow Crocodile,'' he told her, avoiding her eyes. ''You know that.''

''Oh, yes. That was pretty obvious.'' She looked at him over the rim of her coffee cup. She loved him and she wanted him to feel that he could tell her anything. She was going to be very careful not to overreact to anything he said. If she could manage to keep things on a lighthearted level, she would come out ahead. ''In fact, you did such a good job there were times when I was pretty sure you didn't like me much.''

''I didn't,'' he agreed. ''There were times when I couldn't stand you.'' His grin softened his words. ''But I was crazy about you just the same, and you know it.''

She looked thoughtful. "Which, of course, is why you had to act as though you thought I was a prime candidate for *The Gong Show*."

He shrugged, leaning back in his chair. "Sure."

"You see, that's the part I don't get." She put down her cup and leaned forward. "Why did we have to pretend for so long?"

His blue eyes clouded. "Because you were right from the beginning, Lisa. We're incompatible—in what we want, what we need. We should have stayed away from each other."

He still felt that way, after the night they had just had? She could hardly believe it. "Are you really so afraid of commitment?" she asked softly.

He swore under his breath, turning to look at her with exasperation in his eyes. "Forget the 'commitment' bugaboo, Lisa. That's not it. That's never been it. It's just as you pointed out from the first. I want one thing, you want another. We can have some good times. But we don't have a . . . a future, so to speak."

She was trembling. All her good intentions were crumbling. She wanted to wring his neck. "Don't worry, Carson," she said, her voice not concealing the evidence of bitterness. "I'm not trying to trap you into a life with marriage and children. I would never do that."

Reaching out, he took her hand in his, wishing he could express to her what he really meant, knowing his words so far had made him sound like a selfish jerk. "Well, that's good. Then we don't have anything to worry about."

She yanked her hand away from his. "No," she retorted. "Everything is just hunky-dory." Rising, she glared at him and turned. "I'm going to go get dressed," she announced. "I'm going to have to run home and see what kind of damage there's been and then get to work."

He watched her go, kicking himself for the clumsy way he had tried to explain his feelings. She didn't understand. She didn't see what he was really afraid of. The thing that frightened him the most was his own vulnerability. What would happen if he fell in love—if he couldn't live without her—if he was worthless when she wasn't around? He'd already found himself totally out of control around her. What if it got worse? What would he do? For the first time in his life, he was afraid that might really happen.

But he couldn't tell her that.

His doorbell rang and he went to open the door. Outside in the drizzle stood Michi Ann, dressed in a yellow rain-slicker, her dark eyes peering out from under the visor. She had a big paper bag in her hand, and from the sound of it, there was something inside that wanted to get out.

"Hi, mister," she said sadly. She sniffed and tears welled in her eyes. "Could you do me a favor, mister?"

He looked down at the brown paper bag and groaned inwardly, but tried to hide it from her with a smile. "What can I do for you, Michi?"

She held out the bag. "Could you take care of Jake for me?"

Carson swallowed hard, looking at the bag. He made no move to take it from her. "Uh, why? Where are you going?" For the first time, he noticed the tears. "Hey, what's the matter? Come on in and tell me what's wrong."

She came in and stood dripping in his entryway, looking up at him, her eyes glistening. "We're going to Hawaii to see my Grandma," she said, her sobs like tiny hiccups between sentences. "Momma says I can't take Jake. She was going to take him to the pound...."

"Hey." Carson went down on one knee to get to her level. "Don't you worry. I'll take care of him, honey. No one is going to take your best friend to the pound."

"Really, mister?"

What could he say? He would do almost anything for this little girl. "Sure. Why don't you just put him down over there by the stereo?"

She walked over and put the brown paper bag on the floor, then stood back. There was a scrabbling sound. Little by little, the crunched top unwrinkled, and a yellow head poked out of the opening, looking about with fire in its eyes.

Carson rose and stared at the animal. What in God's name was he going to do with the thing? It would take over his entire apartment!

"How long are you going to be gone, Michi?" he asked, dreading the answer.

"Momma says about two weeks. I think." She blinked, staring up at him.

"Two weeks, huh?" Did his hearty voice sound as phony to her as it did to him? "Great. I'll take good care of Jake."

"Thanks, mister. I knew you would help me." Coming up beside him, she put her arms around his knees and put her head against his leg for a quick hug. "You're my best friend, besides Jake."

Leaning down, he dropped a kiss on the top of her head. "You're my pal too, Michi." His voice just a little husky, and there was a tight, hot feeling in his chest. Maybe that icy heart was melting again.

She turned to go, stopping at the door to look back at her cat. She sniffed. "Bye, Jake," she said brokenly. "I'll see you when I get back."

Carson went to the door with her. "Don't worry," he told her. "You'll have a great time in Hawaii. You won't need Jake. You'll be busy meeting relatives and new friends. The time will pass so quickly, you'll feel like you're coming back in no time at all."

"Sure, mister," she answered, with tears welling again. "Bye." And she disappeared out into the rain.

Carson turned and stared at Jake. The cat stared right back.

"Okay," he murmured to himself. "Don't panic. There must be some way to take care of this cat."

But what the hell was he going to do? He'd have to lock it in a room. He'd have to move out and give it the run of the place until Michi got back. And what if she didn't come back?

But, hey. What was wrong with him? He couldn't wimp out like this. He was a man, wasn't he? He'd have to face this animal down, show him who was boss.

Squaring his shoulders, he held the cat's gaze. There was nothing so hard about this. All he had to do was walk over and grab the animal by the scruff of the neck and let it know how the pecking order worked in this place.

"Okay, Jake," he began sternly. "It's just you and me." And he took a step toward where the cat still sat in the bag.

Lisa entered the room at the same moment. "Oh, what a pretty kitty!" She scooped the cat up in her arms and cooed to it. "I didn't know you had any pets," she said brightly, her temper of a few moments earlier back under control. "What a nice cat."

"I don't." Carson stared at Jake's eyes. They blinked contentedly, and the purring could have deafened at ten paces. "This is Michi Ann's cat. You remember the little girl I introduced you to at Kramer's? She asked me to take care of it for a few weeks while she goes to Hawaii."

"Oh." Lisa gave him a tender look, and he grimaced.

"Now, don't go getting all 'Oh, you're really just an old softee, aren't you?' on me because it isn't like that at all. The truth is, I hate this cat. And he hates me."

"This sweet baby?"

"That evil changeling, you mean. He's a killer. Believe me."

She looked down at the limp animal in her arms. It looked back with adoring eyes. "Right. Do you want me to take him home? I bet I could reform him."

Wouldn't that be great? For just a moment, Carson thought he might have found his salvation. But then he shook his head. "No. I promised to take care of him. I don't want to let Michi Ann down."

"Okay."

She released the cat and turned to look at him. "Are you going to give me a ride home?" she asked briskly. "I think it's time I got going."

He stared at her. Well, wasn't this what he wanted—a backing away, a bit of distance, some perspective on it all? She was cool, calm, and just as sexy as ever.

Throwing all his good intentions to the wind, he stepped up and took her into his arms. "That's where you made your first mistake," he whispered, kissing her neck, her earlobe, her cheek. "It's not time to get going at all."

She felt her knees weaken and she smiled. He might pretend to regret their new relationship, but when it came right down to it, he was just as happy with it was she was. "Oh, yeah? What *is* it time for, then?"

He grinned and nibbled at the corners of her mouth. There was no point in answering that with words. He let his body say it all.

Nine

"We reopen one week from today."

Lisa sat very still, her mind numb as Greg went on describing the opening ceremony for Loring's Family Center. Her dream was coming to fruition. Now they would find out whether she was a winner or a failure. It all boiled down to that.

She took a drink of the water she kept beside her at the conference table these days. Her mouth always seemed to be so dry. Stress, she told herself. She was certainly under pressure.

Looking down the table, she winked at Carson, and he raised an eyebrow her way. It had been weeks since they had finally admitted how they felt about each other and begun to see each other regularly. Weeks of heaven. Weeks of hell.

She stood and looked up and down the table at her entire staff and Carson. She smiled. "I want to thank you all for what you've done over the last few weeks. We've all worked so hard, and we're about to find out if it's all been worthwhile. I hope it has. Our futures depend on it. As well as our past." She smiled and nodded toward the portrait of her grandfather. "Win or lose, I want you all to know how much I appreciate your extra efforts. And if things go well, I hope to reward you accordingly. Thank you again."

There were so many last-minute details to take care of. The day-care center for the employees was off and running, and the child-care center for customers was still in the planning stages. Lisa spent a lot of time on those plans, in addition to visiting the employees' area to get new ideas. She dropped in a couple of times a day to play with the children. Garrison's Becky was the star attraction. Everyone wanted to hold the darling little girl. More than once, Lisa had looked up from a session with the children to find Carson watching her from the doorway, his expression flat and unreadable.

"I don't know why no one thought to do this years ago," she told him later that day as they walked past the room where the children were, their squeals loud enough to penetrate the thick walls. "It stands to reason that a mother who knows her child is being taken care of properly will be a better worker. I'm sure morale has improved. Why wasn't it been done before? It's only logical."

"Female logical," he teased.

She grinned. "Female logic is the ingredient that keeps the world on an even keel," she pointed out. "Don't you know anything?"

They were together every moment they could be. She didn't want to be blatant in front of the staff, but she couldn't stay away from him any more than he could stay away from her. They grabbed stolen moments at her house, at his apartment, in the car. They seemed to have an insatiable hunger for each other, as if they were making up for lost time. There were days when a deprivation of only a few hours would lead them to take things to ridiculous extremes.

A case in point had been the night before at the Duprees' indoor swim party. The house was fabulous and included a glassed-in swimming pool that overlooked the valley and had a panoramic view of the ocean. You could see the ships passing far out to sea, watch the light come on in the lighthouse at the end of the jetty, hear the waves, and at the same time, tread lovely warm water and sip cocktails insulated from the weather, or soak up relaxation in the hot tub.

Lisa had worn a one-piece swimsuit that she thought was modest enough. A bright electric blue, it was high-cut but covered just about everything that ought to be covered quite thoroughly. It was only after she'd noticed the men of the party spending an awful lot of time waiting for her to emerge from the water that she realized her mistake. Wet, the fabric clung and enhanced her best features. One look at Carson's face confirmed it. Embarrassed, she headed for the dressing rooms.

There were two rows of changing cubicles—men on one side, women on the other. She went into the last stall and shimmied out of her wet suit, dropping it to the ground, and picked up one of the fluffy white guest towels to rub her hair dry. A sound from behind stopped her. She spun around.

"Carson!" she gasped.

"Hush." He put a finger to his lips and reached behind to lock the compartment door, his glazed eyes taking in her round bare breasts, her slender waist, her long, tanned legs. She stared at him, recognizing the white-hot look in his eyes.

"Carson, no," she whispered. "Not here."

He smiled and pulled her to him, his palm beginning a slow massage on her nipple, drawing it high and hard. "Why not?" he said softly. "The rest of them are otherwise occupied. They'll never know."

She was easy to persuade. His hands knew the shortcuts to her desire. "I have no backbone at all," she murmured.

"Interesting," he whispered into her ear. "Maybe we should explore some new positions."

Her laugh bubbled low in her throat and she reached out to help him get rid of the swimming trunks, then bent back across the dressing table as he explored his opportunities.

Making love with Carson was always new. He found new ways to touch her, new places to excite her, new things that drove her mad with a hunger to have him inside her. His white heat became hers, and she moaned softly, moving her hips and wanting him, needing him, drawing him in to renew the bond that held them as closely as any other.

"Lisa?"

Everything came to a crashing stop as a voice from outside the cubicle penetrated their growing frenzy. Lisa's eyes opened wide and she held her breath.

"Lisa? It's Andy Douglas. I know you're in there. I heard your voice."

She looked desperately up into Carson's eyes but he was going on as though he hadn't heard a thing.

"Lisa, listen. I just had the greatest idea. This party is about to wind down. How would you like to go out in my new Rolls and take a spin through the countryside? We could take the bluff road up to Cally's Overpass and look at the city lights. We could even drive down to Santa Barbara and visit a nice little tearoom I know of. What do you say?"

Lisa couldn't have said anything if she'd wanted to. Carson was in control, and he'd brought her to the point of no return. She closed her eyes and bit down on his shoulder to keep from crying out. She was vaguely aware that he had grunted in response, but she was beyond caring. She was one with him again, where she longed to be for now, forever, for always.

"They do have the nicest little sandwiches. Watercress, I think. Or maybe cucumber. I know you would love this place."

She lay back panting. Carson looked down at her, laughing.

"I'm going to get you for this," she mouthed at him. "I can't believe..."

"We could drive back along the coast. There's a quaint little fishing village down a long dirt road near Camino Corto. I'd love to show it to you."

She struggled to her feet and began pulling on her clothing, muttering as she worked. Carson merely slipped into his trunks and was decent again.

"Lisa? Lisa?"

She threw a scathing look Carson's way and took a deep breath, throwing open the door and marching out with her head held high. "I'm sorry, Andy," she told him, trying to smile. "It's awfully nice of you to invite me, but I'm afraid I'm going to be busy tonight."

"Darn," he said. Then his eyes widened as Carson came out behind her. He took in their flushed cheeks, their rumpled clothing, and put two and two together. "Oh, gee. Well, if that's the way it is..."

She smiled at him. "That's the way it is. I'm sorry."

As they walked away she muttered to Carson in a soft but steely voice, "If you ever do something like that to me again, I'll kill you!"

"You attack me the way you just did in there," he retorted, "and I'll die a happy man."

* * *

The next afternoon, he came into her office when she was working on financial reports. "Leave the door open," she said, looking at him sideways.

He complied, looking around to see her reason. "Why?" he asked when he didn't get the point.

"Because I want to make sure you don't get any ideas."

Swinging around, he grinned down at her. "I was born with ideas," he told her. "In fact—" he settled down in a chair and looked at her almost seriously "—I've got a really good one right now."

She took off her glasses and gazed at him suspiciously. "Dare I ask what that might be?"

His blue eyes regarded her warmly. "God, you look pretty in the morning," he complimented instead of answering. "Did you know that? Do you plan that? Or are you just naturally—"

"Carson," she broke in warningly. "Tell me what your idea is. I don't want to find out in the middle of a meeting or something."

"Okay," he relented, just a little grumpily. "You don't ever let me have any fun."

Her eyes flashed. "The idea?"

"Okay, okay. Guess what? Ben Capalletti is taking his wife and oldest daughter and oldest son to San Francisco overnight this weekend."

"Carson, we don't have time to go to San Francisco—"

"I know that. Let me finish. I overhead Ben calling around, trying to find a baby-sitter for the four little tots he's leaving behind."

"Oh?"

"Imagine his shock and surprise when I volunteered."

She blinked. "Imagine mine."

He looked very pleased with himself. "As you might guess, I have an ulterior motive."

She almost laughed aloud. Mr. No-Kids-in-My-Life was volunteering to baby-sit. "No doubt."

He leaned forward and looked directly into her eyes. "You talk a good game, lady. You think you're so hot to have a family. Let's see what happens when you test-drive one."

She frowned. He must be joking. "You mean?"

His eyes were dancing with mischief. "I mean dirty diapers. I mean feeds at two in the morning and whiny kids with runny noses." He reached across the desk and stroked her cheek with the back of his hand. "It's time to fish or cut bait, my dear. I'm talking real babies. Not cute little just-washed numbers gurgling in fancy carriers like you get at the child-care center."

He really meant it. She gazed at him speculatively. He was setting her up for a scenario with disaster and hoping she would see the error of her dreams. What if he was successful? Her fighting spirit came to the surface. No, she was going to show him. She could take anything those little babies might have to offer. Bring on the kids!

He was still babbling on. "This is going to be flesh and dirt, and maybe blood." One eyebrow rose. "Think you can handle it?"

Hah! Just stand back and give her room. She gave him her rendition of a snappy military salute. "I'll do my best, sir."

His grin was smug and self-satisfied. "I think I'm going to enjoy this. The disillusionment of Lisa Loring."

Her returning smile was just as smug. "Maybe." He had no doubts. She could see that.

Reconsidering, he leaned forward again. "Listen to me. I'll make you a deal." He took her hand in his and held it, looking at her with a tender, sympathetic smile that made her want to throttle him. "If this helps you decide that maybe babies are something you don't really want to mess with after all..." His eyes deepened and he hesitated, then said softly, "Come to Tahiti with me."

She hadn't expected that. Her pulse quickened. "But you only have one ticket," she reminded him, putting off answering.

"I'd trade that in for a slow boat to China if you'd just come with me."

His words filled her soul like hot buttered rum on a cold night. She would love to go to Tahiti with him. But that wasn't the sort of promise she was looking for. She had to hold out for the real thing. He wanted her now. But for how long? She knew he wasn't guaranteeing anything.

"I'll take you up on the baby-sitting experiment," she said at last. "But as for Tahiti..." She shrugged.

He nodded, not pressuring her. "Okay. Saturday night. Don't forget."

How could she forget? He reminded her of it every time she saw him. But finally the night came, and she went over to the Capalletti's house with trepidation.

It started out calmly enough. The Capallettis had a lovely home on a bluff overlooking the ocean. Carson introduced her to each child in turn, and she visited each of their beautifully decorated rooms. She looked through the clothes in the two-year-old's room, and in the nursery. What adorable little things—the little bonnets, the tiny booties, the cute pacifier. Everything seemed so cute and so new to her. These lovely children, their beautiful home— how could Carson have thought this visit would turn her off children?

Things only started to go bad after the baby started to fuss.

"What do you suppose he wants?" she asked Carson worriedly.

"Your guess is as good as mine," he answered, staying aloof. "I don't speak their language."

She tried to play with the baby, tried to distract him, but the fussing was getting louder and louder, and she began to worry. What if something was really wrong? How could she tell what the baby needed when he couldn't give her the words?

Carson did offer to heat up a bottle, but the baby rejected it with a lemon face and began to cry in earnest.

"Quick," Carson said, examining the puckered little face. "Before that turns into a howl like you won't believe—start walking him."

"Walking him?" She had visions of leashes and fire hydrants, but he quickly dispelled those notions.

"This is what you do. You throw him over your shoulder and you walk back and forth for hours. Believe me. Once you start, they never let you stop again. They love it."

"But . . . how can I take care of the other children if I'm walking the baby?"

He beamed at her. "You're beginning to catch on."

She walked the baby. Actually, he felt rather wonderful snuggled up against her shoulder. Just to smell the sweet scent of that little head was almost worth the effort. But Carson was right. Once she started, the baby wouldn't let her stop. Whenever she even slowed down, he would begin to fuss again. So she walked through the house, into the yard, back in through the kitchen—and that was when she had her run-in with twelve-year-old Billy. Billy wore a baseball bat over his shoulder as though it were a permanent piece of clothing, making her jump every time he turned around near something breakable. She caught him moving toward the back door.

"Where do you think you're going?" she asked as pleasantly as she could with a fifteen-pound baby on her shoulder.

"Out to play." He looked at her levelly.

That didn't seem right. "It's after dark."

His eyes were cool and confident. "Mom always lets me."

Could that really be? She appealed to Carson, who was watching from the doorway. He shook his head.

She turned back to the boy. "I'm sorry, but I don't feel comfortable with letting you outside to play after dark. You'll have to wait until your mother comes home and ask her."

Horror radiated from his face. "But that will be tomorrow."

She wavered, but in the end she held firm. "Right."

He shifted tactics. "Then, since I don't have anything else to do, can we rent a video?"

"No."

His lower lip was beginning to protrude. "Why not?"

"Because we are too busy."

"I'm not."

Good answer. She had to think of something fast. "Want a job? There are dishes to do."

He didn't bother to answer such a ridiculous question. "Can I have some friends stay over night?" he countered instead.

"I don't think you better do that tonight."

"Why not?"

She had to swallow and count to ten before she could answer sweetly, "Because I said so. Now, why don't you run along..."

"Can I move the TV into my room?"

Oh, Lord. He never quit. And now the baby was kicking, complaining because she wasn't walking. "I don't know," she replied a little desperately. "Does your mother let you do that?"

"Sure. All the time."

Carson came to the rescue. "Don't believe him for one minute," he said, walking into the room shaking his head.

Billy threw Carson a look of disgust and gave up, stomping fiercely from the room.

Lisa frowned. "I don't know. You practically called him a liar to his face."

Carson grinned. "He is a liar."

Lisa was aghast. "But he's a nice boy—"

"Sure, he is. And he'll grow up to be a fine, upstanding pillar of the community. But right now he's twelve. Reality doesn't exist for him. And he'll say anything to get a TV in his room."

Lisa looked at Carson, amused. Did he realize how much he knew about raising children? It all seemed to be coming back to him now that he was among them this way.

"Why don't we all gather together in the den and watch television?" she suggested. "It would be like a real family gathering."

"Yup," he agreed. "A gathering of the Adams family." He shook his head. "Don't do it. You'll regret it."

She shifted the baby from one shoulder to the other and stretched out her arm to get the circulation going again. It seemed like a good idea to her. A warm, cozy picture formed in her mind—the children in their jammies all cuddled up and everyone eating popcorn. "But why?"

He looked at her, amused by how little she knew. When you came right down to it, he was the expert after all his years of handling his aunt's clan. He'd forgotten how much he remembered. To tell the truth, he was sort of pleased with his instincts in these matters. It never hurt to have experience.

"It's a nice theory," he explained to her patiently, "but it doesn't work. You see, babies don't watch TV. And one of their main pleasures in life is ruining TV-watching for others. And two-year-olds don't really watch TV. They yell at it. They throw things at it. They might even go up and kiss the screen. But they don't watch it." He was enjoying himself. "So what does that leave you with? The seven-year-old who will want cartoons. And the twelve-year-old who will want to watch *Crime Cracker Cops*. And how about us?" Narrowing his eyes, he looked at her. "Do we turn our minds to mush with cartoons, or fry our brains with *Crime Cracker Cops*?"

Her eyes lit up. "*Casablanca*'s on tonight. Maybe..."

He shook his head. "Not a chance. They'll make mincemeat out of you. They have no mercy."

He was probably right. He did seem to know a lot about kids, and rather than standing back and laughing at her mistakes, he was with her every step of the way, giving advice, actually getting in on the action. She was impressed.

When C.C., the two-year-old, threw the car keys down the toilet, Carson was the one who retrieved them. When Deanie, the seven-year-old girl, gave all teenage Holly's stuffed animals a haircut, Carson used Ben's electric razor to even out the cut and then he even cleaned up the mess. And in the end, he walked the baby so she could put the others to bed.

Billy was the one who asked for a bedtime story, surprising her. She managed to think up something with fights and daring adventures rather than princesses and castles.

While she told it, Carson watched her from the doorway with the baby asleep on his shoulder. He stood quietly and listened to her voice. Conflicting emotions were tugging at him, struggling for the upper hand. His plan had been to overwhelm her with kids and how much trouble they were. But she'd taken to caring for them as though she'd been doing it all her life. What could he do? She was a natural-born nurturer. How could he try to take that away from her if that was what she really wanted? It was what she was made for.

He looked at the boy falling asleep in his baseball cap, and suddenly thought of his own childhood. What he had told Lisa about it had been true, as far as it went. But he had neglected to put his father into the picture. Standing here now, looking at this young boy, he remembered the times his father had been there, between prison terms. His father had tucked him in and told him stories and taken him to baseball games. Funny how he'd forgotten all about that. Why had he pushed it into the recesses of his mind all these years? His father had done things with him when he was able to. Still, all these years he had harbored this deep-seated anger at his father, for deserting him, for going off to jail and leaving him behind with Aunt Flo. Suddenly he realized that the anger had been that much deeper because the times with his father had been so good. He couldn't accept that they had been snatched from him the way they were. He couldn't accept that his father had done things that caused the good times to end. Maybe it was time he reassessed a lot of things.

Lisa was the one who was supposed to be doing the re-appraisal. He'd brought her here to prove to her that she really didn't want what she thought she wanted. Instead, he was getting a revelation of his own. His plan had back-fired.

The morning was hectic but far from awful. Lisa enjoyed getting breakfast together for so many people, until the fumes from the cooking seemed to get to her.

"You're looking a little green around the gills," Carson remarked, taking the spatula from her and making her sit down.

She took a deep breath and looked away from the food. "I've got kind of an upset stomach."

"Oh, yeah?" He looked concerned. "Is it something you ate?"

She swallowed hard and avoided his eyes. "No, I just... you know, I think it's the stress. I've been feeling a little funny ever since we decided to go ahead with the Family Center idea. It's just the pressure...."

He stroked her hair. "Oh. Sure. Well, why don't you take something? I'm sure Ben has something in the medicine cabinet."

"No, no," she said quickly. "Oh, no. I couldn't take anything."

He turned and looked at her, his eyes dark. "Why not?"

"Because—well, uh, I never do. I hate to take things like that."

He stood still for a moment, then shrugged and left to go help Jeremy find his basketball. Lisa walked out into the hall and looked at herself in the mirror. Slowly, she raised her hand to her face and pressed it to her cheek. Was she ever going to admit it, even to herself? This wasn't just stress. Her whole body was changing. What if—what if she was pregnant?

It seemed impossible at first. After all, she'd been so careful. But there had been that very first time....

A visit to the doctor a couple of days later confirmed it.

"Yes, I believe you're a little under a month along," he told her. "What are you planning to do?"

She was startled. "What do you mean?"

"Well, I know you're not married. And you are thirty-five. It's a serious decision."

A serious decision. Her mind was whirling. She couldn't keep it straight. She was pregnant with Carson's baby and she couldn't tell him. She couldn't tell anyone.

How ironic it all seemed. She now had what she'd wanted so badly. But not this way. The two things she had wanted most in the world were within her grasp. But in order to have one of them, she would have to give up the other.

She loved Carson. She was wildly, madly in love with Carson. She needed him as much as she needed air to breathe. But she couldn't go to him pregnant. He'd made it very clear that a baby was something he would never accept. She couldn't do that to him.

At the same time, she wanted her baby, needed it with a deep and fundamental craving that was impossible to deny. And now that she had conceived this child, she had a responsibility to care for it and love it the way it deserved. And that meant giving up Carson.

Giving up Carson—she couldn't stand it! Her body was addicted to him. How could she live without him?

He came to her house for dinner that evening, bringing along cartons of Chinese food so she wouldn't have to cook. She felt like a traitor, keeping such a secret to herself. But what could she do?

Worse, what would he want her to do about it? She didn't even want to think that one through.

They made love and walked on the beach and she pushed the knowledge of what was going on inside her away, pretending there was nothing new, laughing with him, talking as though everything were just the same as it had always been. And every moment that went by without her telling him the truth, she felt as though a tiny piece of her soul were dying.

A baby. His baby. Would it be a boy? Would it look like him? This should be the happiest period of her life. Instead, she felt as though the weight of the world were on her shoulders.

And then, just before going to sleep, Carson reminded her that he would be leaving soon.

"You know I'm leaving for Tahiti right after the opening," he said, and then he took her in his arms. "Will you come with me?"

He asked even though he knew the answer. She turned and tried to smile. "I would love to come with you. You know that."

"But you can't," he answered for her, and something close to anger lit his eyes.

She nodded, her voice too choked to speak.

He turned away and stared out into the blackness of the ocean. Despair shivered through his soul. He didn't know what he was going to do without her. Should he stay?

No. He couldn't stay. Staying would be the same as promising her things that would never be. It would be a lie to stay. He had to go.

She looked up, wondering why he wasn't saying anything. He was so still, so cold. She knew he was troubled, but she wasn't sure why. Should she tell him? What would he do if he knew?

No, she couldn't. She could never trap him that way. She'd promised she wouldn't. She would keep her promise.

Suddenly he swung back toward her. "I'm leaving," he told her, his voice almost angry. "And I've got that damn cat at my place. Will you be able to take him?"

Michi Ann still wasn't back. According to Jan, Carson's neighbor, she would be back in a few more days. But in the meantime, he'd had to take care of Jake. They had established an uneasy truce. One of Carson's proudest moments had been when he'd ordered Jake into the bedroom, and Jake had gone, tail dragging along the floor. From then on, things had begun to change. Now they were almost friends. In some stupid way he was actually going to miss the crazy animal.

"Of course, I'll take Jake," she said. She took a deep breath. "I hope you have a good trip."

He turned and stared at her. Neither one of them could manage a smile. They both knew they were in for heartbreak, no matter what happened.

Maybe that was just the price you had to pay, she thought to herself as she stared into the darkness of the room after he'd turned out the light. But would she have given up having him for the past month in order to spare herself this pain?

Never.

The opening of the store was a tremendous success. The people of San Feliz might like to go to Kramer's to see what was new, but they went to Loring's to get what they wanted. Lisa was pleased, but her old goal to beat out Mike seemed juvenile now.

She planned to hand the reins of power over to Greg. She'd discussed her decision with Carson and he agreed with her. So the success was sweet, but almost irrelevant. She had more pressing problems now. She was pregnant, and the man she loved was about to walk out of her life.

Carson was leaving. That phrase echoed in her head, pounding like a drum. She didn't know if she could bear it.

They spent one last night together. She tried to laugh and joke and make it a special occasion, but the tears were so close to the surface, she had to be very careful. She kept thinking about the life beginning inside her. She should tell him, she kept thinking. My God, he was going to leave and she hadn't told him.

They made love and as they lay back upon the pillows, she made her decision. Despite everything, he had to know.

She had just taken in a deep breath and was prepared to do what frightened her the most, when he surprised her.

"I'm not going to Tahiti," he said.

She stopped where she was, white with shock. "No?"

He shook his head. "At least not now. I'm going to Kansas. I'm going to see my father."

She searched his eyes. There was very little bitterness left in them. "Oh, Carson, I'm so glad."

"I thought you would be." Cupping her face in his hands, he kissed her lips. "You ought to be. It's because of you that I'm going."

She got up and went to the window. The night was clear and a silver moon sailed over the black ocean. How could she tell him now? She couldn't do anything to keep him from going to reconcile with his father.

"I still wish you would think about coming with me, Lisa," he continued. "I could stop for you on my way back."

She shook her head, staring out at the water. "No. I can't leave. There are things I have to take care of here."

He came up behind her and took her in his arms. "I want you to know," he murmured, "that I've never felt like this about anyone else. You've changed my life, Lisa. I'll never forget you."

She smiled as tears welled in her eyes. So she was like her mother, after all. A lot of good it had done her. She'd changed a casual playboy into a caring man, but she hadn't changed his need to wander. As the song said, he had to be free.

"I love you, Carson," she whispered brokenly.

He answered with a kiss, making her realize he had never spoken those words back to her. And now he never would.

Ten

Carson had been gone for over a week when Michi Ann finally showed up for her cat. Lisa opened her front door one day, and there she was.

"Hi," she began solemnly, gazing up from under straight-cut bangs. "Auntie Jan said you had Jake. Thank you for taking care of him. Could I have him back now, please?"

"Well, that depends." Lisa smiled at the little girl. She was such an adorable blend of childlike innocence and direct wisdom. "Something has happened. Maybe you'd better come and see."

She led Michi into the house and back to the utility porch where Jake had staked out a place. Drawing back a curtain, Lisa revealed the fat yellow cat lying on a pillow with six tiny kittens squirming around him...er, her. The golden eyes looked up at the little girl and blinked in smug satisfaction.

"Finally," said Michi Ann happily, crossing her arms over her chest.

Lisa raised her eyebrows. "You knew this cat was a female?"

The eyes were huge and candid. "Sure. Jake is short for Jacqueline."

Sure. The most natural thing in the world. Lisa shook her head. "Then why did you refer to her as 'him' all the time?"

The little girl shrugged. "I don't know. It was what everybody else did. I didn't think about it."

Lisa laughed. Reaching out, she lightly touched the girl's silky hair. "Well, if you want to take them, you're going to have to get a box or something."

Michi frowned, then her face lit up. "I have a cart in the car. Auntie Jan just got it for my doll at the thrift shop. It'll be perfect."

She ran out to get her new toy and came back with a rickety doll carriage with a pink pillow and a faded yellow card that said Baby Aboard flapping from the handle. Lisa stared at it, hardly crediting what her eyes were seeing, and then she began to laugh. "I don't believe it," she murmured, but when she thought about it, it seemed perfectly logical. After all the weeks it had resided in front of her house, she was glad it was finally going to **a go**od home. And it certainly was handy for carrying a large yellow cat and six tiny baby kittens.

She waved goodbye to Michi Ann and went back inside. She was moving in a dream these days, completely focused on the gestation occurring inside her. Carson was gone. She would have to forget about him. But she had the baby. And as the days slipped by, that became more and more important to her.

She had been so sure Carson would write, or maybe even telephone. But there had been no word at all, and as time passed, she accepted that. It broke her heart, but a clean break was best, of course.

She spent a lot of time walking on the beach. It was good exercise, they told her. And it gave her a lot of time to think. And time to talk to the new life inside her.

The baby was growing. Her stomach was beginning to protrude. She found herself with one hand on the new roundness most of the time, as though waiting for something to happen in there, some communication from the gestational world. She wasn't sure just what she was expecting. Morse code, perhaps? But she talked to the baby a lot, and when it was ready to talk back, she was going to be ready to listen.

She'd changed so much since she'd come to San Feliz. She'd fallen in love. She'd conceived a baby. She'd saved a business. All in all, it had been a very good year.

That was the way she was trying to look at it. What else could she do?

She tried not to think about Carson. He would always be her baby's father, but from now on, he was part of their past. The more firmly she kept him there, the better off they would be.

And so, when she picked up the telephone and heard his voice one evening a few weeks later, she fought hard to keep the tears that splashed from her eyes out of her voice as she talked to him. It was wonderful to hear from him. But at the same time, she knew it only meant she would have to get over the immediacy of losing him all over again.

They talked softly and she curled up in the chair, as though she could somehow hold him that way. He told her about his father, how they had been making up for lost time, getting to know each other, discovering so much about each other, about themselves.

"I feel like a new man," he said. "Reborn. I'm starting all over again. And it's all because of you, Lisa."

She swallowed hard and didn't dare risk a reply.

His voice softened. "I'm leaving for Tahiti on Saturday."

She still didn't answer, and he hesitated.

"Lisa," he said at last, and there was something different in his tone. "Change your mind. Come with me."

It seemed as though minutes rolled by, hours, before she could breathe again. "I can't, Carson," she managed at last, struggling not to show the turmoil she felt in her voice. "I'm sorry."

He was quiet for so long, she almost thought he might have dropped the phone and left the room. But when he finally spoke again, he sounded almost normal.

"Well, listen, my flight goes through San Francisco around noon, and I have a two hour layover. How about driving up and going out to lunch with me?" His tone grew slightly husky as he added, "I'd love to see you."

This was pure torture. She ached to run to him, ached to tell him yes, yes, anything he wanted, yes! But she couldn't. She had to be strong.

For the baby, she told herself, placing her hand over her stomach. For the baby.

"Saturday?" she said with false brightness. "Oh, I'm sorry Carson, but I have plans for Saturday. I'm afraid I can't make it."

His voice was hard. "You could make it if you wanted to."

She closed her eyes. "Yes," she admitted softly. "Carson, I'm just trying to do what is best for both of us."

"Of course." He was silent for a moment, then went on. "I hope you find someone someday who deserves you, Lisa," he said completely without irony. "You're really special. I... I miss you like crazy."

Tears were welling in her eyes and her throat was too choked to speak. She tried to say his name, but no sound would come out of her mouth.

"Goodbye, Lisa. Stay well. I love you."

She gasped as the phone clicked in her ear. He'd hung up. He'd said he loved her, and then he had hung up. "Carson?" she cried into the receiver. But he was gone.

For a moment she was desperate to find out what his number was so she could call him back, but she quickly calmed down. It was no use. She'd found out that *love* didn't solve everything. Still, she hugged the word to her for the rest of the night, and at the same time, she told herself over and over how proud she was of her own will to not give in to temptation and run to him. It was for the best. It was for the baby.

That belief sustained her for the next few days. She seemed to need to sleep for hours and hours, almost as though she were blocking thought from her mind. And then, Friday evening, as she was lying in her bed, just about to doze off once again, she felt something move.

Both hands went to her stomach and she held her breath. There it was again. She'd felt a fluttering before, like butterflies dancing inside her, but this was more. This was firm, even slightly grumpy. The baby had finally kicked.

Joy spilled through her, an ecstasy like nothing she had ever known before. The miracle overwhelmed her. Her baby... Carson's baby... was real, it was here. She had to share this sensation, this feeling with him. She had to.

She told herself she was crazy. The argument in her head grew louder and louder as she dashed through her house, making preparations to drive up to San Francisco in the morning, but she wouldn't listen. She had to make one last try. She owed it to herself. She owed it to Carson.

She decided on a lime green suit with a boxy jacket that would hide her new bulk. At the first light of morning, she got into her car and started toward the highway. By late morning, she was finding a parking space in the airport parking structure.

She spotted him right away in the crowd debarking the flight from the Midwest. He looked tired, a bit rumpled, but when he saw her, his face lit up, and she flew into his arms.

"You look beautiful," he said when he had finished kissing every inch of her face and neck. "Being away from me must be good for you. You've gained weight."

She pulled back and tugged at the hem of her jacket, suddenly self-conscious. "Let's find somewhere private where we can talk," she said, looking around the terminal. "I have something I want to say to you."

"Me too," he told her, slipping an arm around her shoulders. "How about one of those dark little restaurants they seem to have all along the way here? We'll ask for a table at the back."

They found the perfect place, got settled and ordered, laughing all the while. The waitress was helpful, giving them all the privacy possible and bringing the food quickly, then withdrawing to leave them in peace.

Lisa was so happy to see Carson, everything seemed funny and full of joy. But finally they were alone, and it was time. Her heart started to beat very quickly in her chest.

There was a silent pause while they both avoided each other's eyes.

"Carson, I..."

"Lisa, listen..."

They both started at once, and stopped, laughing.

"You go first, " she urged. "I can wait."

"You're sure?"

She nodded.

"Okay." He took a deep breath. "Here it is in a nutshell. I don't want to go to Tahiti."

Lisa stared at him. "What?"

He met her gaze ruefully. "It's true. I kept looking at my ticket this past week or so and thinking...how much more I would rather be wherever you are than go to Tahiti." He held up a hand. "Now wait. Let me get it all out. I...you see, I've always thought I just naturally had a restless soul, that I had to move on no matter what, that I would never want to stay in one place for long. But something has changed, and now I realize, that wasn't it at all."

She nodded, encouraging him to go on, holding her breath.

Reaching out, he took her hand. "I was searching for something, Lisa. And...I don't feel like I have to go searching for it any longer."

"Carson...." She couldn't choke out anything more than his name.

"Wait. I know I'm not the man of your dreams. I know I'm not anything like the man you've been looking for to make your life the way you want it. But I want to stay near you, Lisa. Would—could you stand it?" His eyes were dark with vulnerability and she bit her lip and closed her eyes before she answered.

"Lisa," he said, his voice trembling with emotion. "Would you like to marry me?"

She nodded, her eyes brimming with tears. "Only, I do have one condition," she warned him. "I know you've said you don't like children, but... I'm going to have to have one. At least one. You see—"

Taking her face between his hands, he kissed her soundly on the mouth. "Oh Lisa, I don't care. Go ahead and have ten children. I'll deal with it when it comes up."

"Uh..." She tried to smile, even though she felt just as much like crying. "We're getting married?"

He kissed her again. "Lisa, Lisa, yes." His eyes were shining and he gazed at her tenderly. "I want nothing more in this world than to marry you."

The tears began to spill down from her eyes, but she wasn't finished yet. "Well, there's one more thing," she told him quickly as he reached for her again. "I have a surprise for you. Uh... close your eyes and give me your hand."

"What?"

She took a shuddering breath. "Just do it."

He looked at her for a moment, taking in the tears, the tremulous smile, and his heart filled. Obediently, he closed his eyes and let her take his hand. She took it and carefully placed it... he wasn't sure where. He frowned, trying to figure it out. He felt the linen of her suit and knew it had to be on her body somewhere, but it was rounded in a firm, wide way that he couldn't place.

And then something happened. Something moved under his palm.

"Hey." He jerked his hand back as though it had been burned and opened his eyes. He found himself staring at Lisa's stomach. She sat back with the jacket open and the rounded mound of her stomach sticking up. Carson tried to speak and couldn't. He swallowed and took two quick gulps of air. "You're pregnant," he breathed finally, staring at her.

She nodded, face tense. "Are you angry?" she asked softly, searching his eyes.

"Angry?" He stared at her stomach where he'd felt the movement. Hesitantly, he reached out again. Then he looked into her eyes, his own wide with wonder, and said quietly, as though to convince himself, "We've got a baby. You and me." A smile lit his face. "Why didn't you tell me?"

"I...I was afraid to. I didn't want you to feel trapped. I knew you didn't want children and..."

"Children. Yeah, sure, I don't want quote-children-unquote. But my own baby. Our baby. Don't you understand how different that is?" And he had the nerve to look at her quizzically, completely ignoring the fact that he hadn't understood it himself until he'd felt that little kick bump against his hand.

The baby kicked again and he laughed aloud. "What do you think it is?" he asked her excitedly. "A knee? An elbow?"

She smiled at his enthusiasm. Was it really going to be all right? Was she dreaming? "I think it's a tiny little foot," she said.

Reaching out, she took him in her arms. "Carson James," she said huskily, "I don't know what ever gave you the idea that you were not the man of my dreams. Because you're dead wrong. You're the only man I've ever really loved, and the only man who could possibly complete my life."

His arms wrapped around her and held her close. "Lisa, my darling Lisa," he whispered. "We're going to build a family, you, me and the little one—a family like the one we both always knew was waiting out there for us somewhere."

There was a misty dampness to his eyes, a catch in his voice, and she knew he meant every word. She relaxed in his arms, so full of happiness and wonder she could hardly believe this was real. It had only been hours ago that she had been so sure she had lost him forever. And now—everything she had ever wanted was within her grasp.

"A family," she repeated softly, caressing his cheek with her hand. "That's what we'll make, Carson."

His hand covered hers and he turned to press his lips to her palm, closing his eyes as he held her. "A family," he said again. "Yes. That's a promise."

His hand went to her stomach and cupped the area where the movement had been. She melted against him, laughing softly. *Love* was going to be enough after all.

"Everything okay over here?" asked the waitress, giving the untouched food on their table a quick survey. "Is something wrong? Do you want me to—"

Carson disentangled himself from Lisa's embrace and reached into the pocket of his suit coat. "The food was fine," he reassured her. "But we have to leave." Pulling out his ticket, he laid it on the table along with a large bill to cover the charges. "Want to go to Tahiti?" he asked the waitress as he helped Lisa to her feet. "I'm not going to be able to use this ticket. If you can be ready in an hour, you've got a free trip."

The waitress gasped, picking up the ticket and looking through it quickly. "But where are you going?" she cried.

"Me?" Carson grinned and drew Lisa close to him. "I'm going home."

*   *   *   *   *

SILHOUETTE® Desire™

COMING NEXT MONTH

#679 MARRIAGE, DIAMOND STYLE—Mary Lynn Baxter
Fiery-tempered Matthew Diamond took one look at cool
Brittany Fleming and knew she was trouble. But the opportunity to
thaw the big-city ice princess was one he vowed not to miss!

#680 ANGEL FOR HIRE—Justine Davis
Alexandra Logan's prayers were answered when Michael Justice
appeared to help run her refuge for Vietnam veterans. But
what would she do when she discovered he was an absolute
angel—*literally?*

#681 THE STORMRIDERS—Donna Carlisle
Red Worthington and Meg Forrest didn't believe in love at first sight
until they met each other—and married *immediately!* But would love
be enough once the honeymoon was over?

#682 MISS PRIM—Peggy Moreland
When Jack Brannan called in etiquette expert Malinda Compton to
teach his four sons some manners, *he* learned that in his arms,
Miss Prim wasn't so proper after all!

#683 THE LADY AND THE LUMBERJACK—Jackie Merritt
Christy Allen didn't trust men—especially ones like Vince Bonnell.
But when the handsome lumberjack offered the lady logger a helping
hand, Christy found she couldn't let go....

#684 'TWAS THE NIGHT—Lass Small
December's *Man of the Month,* Bob Brown, swore off women after
his divorce. Until he met feisty Josephine Malone and decided she
was one girl he could take home for the holidays.

AVAILABLE NOW: